# SECRETS SHE KNEW

A SECRETS AND LIES SUSPENSE NOVEL

## D.L. WOOD

SILVERGLASS PRESS

ISBN-13: 979-8-6194-6723-9
First edition
Silverglass Press
Huntsville, Alabama

D.L. Wood
www.dlwoodonline.com
Huntsville, Alabama

# ACKNOWLEDGMENTS

Thank you:

To Shaw Gookin, Kimberly Pugh, Tessa Hobbs, Laura Stratton and Kari Long for being the first to read the manuscript, share your insights and make the book better;

To my editor, Lenda Selph, for her excellent eye and assistance;

To my family and friends for their constant encouragement;

To my readers for their never-ending support; and,

To Ron, for loving me even when I'm in crazy writer mode.

I'm indebted to you all.

*For my sister, Danielle, my partner in crime, who makes me laugh and truly gets me, ALWAYS; and,*

*For my brother, Bobby, who has forever had my back and who would cross an ocean to help me—or a stranger—and has.*

*I love you both.*

# 1

D anielle Lake was fifteen years old the first time she saw a dead body.

July of 1995 in Skye, Alabama, was a brutal summer, full of locusts and blazing heat, withering everything —people, animals and foliage alike. It was the kind of heat that somehow made Dani feel crispy, even though at seventy percent humidity she could pretty much drink the air as much as breathe it.

*Wish I had my stupid driver's license already,* she yearned for the millionth time that week. Then she could drive to Green's Drugs to meet Sasha and Peter instead of riding there on the bicycle she had owned since she was eleven, like some kind of middle-schooler. Dani's gut curdled at the thought of parking her bike in the rack in front of Green's on Main Street for all to see. But there wasn't anything she could do about it. Her birthday was still six months off.

A thick bead of sweat trickled down her brow, and she lifted a hand from the handlebars to brush it away. Her tires ground against the pavement as she steered, thinking of the treats awaiting her at Green's, which, in addition to being a pharmacy and sundries shop, still operated a 1950s-style soda counter serving up root beer floats and malted milkshakes to the small town. The image of a creamy vanilla scoop melting in cold, fizzy soda flashed in her mind, and she pedaled harder.

*If only I was old enough to drive.*

But for now she was stuck on the little yellow bicycle, with its faded, lime-green pea pod decal on the seat and "Sweet Pea" printed in matching glossy finish down the center bar. Dani leaned her weight to the left, turning off her neighborhood street onto the private driveway of one of the homes, then down onto the grass of its side yard, her legs pumping harder on the uneven ground to keep her momentum going. She cut between the house and its neighbor all the way to the rear boundary of their backyards, maneuvering through a thin tree line until finally shooting out onto a wide dirt path.

The earth was dusty from the lack of rain, and a faint cloud of red kicked up in Dani's wake as she traveled the path which made a perpendicular cut across the back of Dr. Beecher's antebellum estate, leading to the river and then to a gravel road that would eventually drop her out two blocks from Green's on the town square.

Going this way, cutting through yards and back paths and along the river, was not the shortest route to Green's. Or the easiest—the gravel road was never fun, especially if a wheel happened to catch a rock and kick it up into her leg. She could have gone the whole way on real roads—ridden down her street to the next and the next and then turned right toward downtown—all smooth and rock-free and a shorter distance. But the one advantage of the back way trumped all of those other things. Because the back way was unpaved and shaded it was cooler, and at ninety-seven degrees at eleven o'clock in the morning, cooler beat faster any day of the week.

The dirt path was sandwiched between Dr. Beecher's fenced-in horse pasture on the left and a field of four-foot-high cornstalks on the right. Dani rolled along, the white wooden pasture fence scrolling by, the sticky breeze fanning her skin, until reaching the path's end where it met the gravel road. She jammed on the brakes and stopped, straddling the bike. It only took a few seconds of being stationary for an opportunistic mosquito to land on her cheek, and she slapped at it, her skin stinging from the strike.

In the pasture, an aged aluminum trough half-full of water rested beneath a massive oak tree ancient enough to have likely witnessed the Civil War. Its wide expanse of branches and deep green leaves provided the only shade in the field, and that and the water were why Smith and Wesson, Dr. Beecher's two horses, stood beneath it. Smith, dapple grey and at least sixteen hands high, and Wesson, smaller, with his shiny, deep auburn coat, looked up at her from their grazing. She clicked her tongue, but when that didn't elicit a response, she called them by name. Unlike most days, when they would amble over to the fence for a pet and possibly a sugar cube, they looked at her, but made no effort to cross the twenty feet to where she stood. The blistering heat had sapped them too.

If it was cooler, she might see if Dr. Beecher was home, see if he would let her take one of the horses for a ride. Dr. Beecher was nice like that. Always had been, ever since he had happened upon her feeding the horses sugar cubes one day when she was ten. They had been friends ever since. He let her ride the horses and taught her how to brush them down. Sometimes he took her fishing with his daughter, even though the girl was much younger than Dani. He was the only one who could help her with her advanced algebra homework the few times she had struggled—and he loaned her books too, big fat ones with fancy leather trim and gold print on the covers. He was a bookworm like her, and, when she had confessed what an oddball she felt like, he had promised her that though it might not feel like it now, being smart would pay off in the long run. It had for him, and he assured her it would for her too. He had even let her do some filing in his office a few times, so she could earn some spending money, and get a feel for what it was like to be a doctor, a career she was considering. So far, she had saved every penny of that extra cash for the car she hoped to buy.

But today was too hot for riding horses. Giving up on them, Dani started to turn left onto the gravel driveway which would carry her down one side of the estate, parallel to the river for a few hundred yards before ending at Main Street. But as she raised her right foot, preparing to shove all her weight on the pedal to get the bike rolling, she spotted something out of the corner of her eye, way off to the right, set back close to the riverbank.

She put her foot back down.

*Honeysuckle.* A vibrant green vine, tucked away under a grove of pines at the river's edge, with fat yellow and white flowers just twenty or so yards away, begging for someone to pull out the sweet stems and sample the nectar inside.

*I've got time,* she considered. *Sasha and Peter won't be at Green's for another half hour.*

Swiveling her handlebars to the right, she started pedaling, crossing over the gravel drive that crunched beneath her wheels until dropping onto the grass beyond. Her bones jarred with every rock and hole the tires met, the bicycle bouncing so much that she had to keep her teeth clamped together, or risk chipping a tooth. A chipped tooth would not only mean pain, but a trip to the dentist, something her parents would not have appreciated, given that they had been living paycheck to paycheck since early May, when her father had blown out his knee playing softball. The doctors said it would be another two months before he could return to work as a mechanic at the auto garage. For now, money was in extra short supply and if she spent any of it by hurting herself while biking off-road to pick honeysuckle, it would be a long time before she would hear the end of it.

Years later, looking back on the whole thing, Dani wouldn't be able to say why the honeysuckle had been so appealing in that moment. It was just honeysuckle, after all. But it was summer and it was something to do and so she did it.

She would spend the rest of her life wishing she hadn't.

The yellow, white, and green leafy curtain ran at least two dozen feet down the barbed wire fence that separated Dr. Beecher's property from the town-owned riverbank. The vines were interwoven and thick, all the way from the burgeoning top, down to the dirt where they piled in mounds. With about ten yards to go, Dani finally hopped off and pushed the bicycle the rest of the way, the handlebars jerking in her hands as she crossed the rough ground. Near the bush, she kicked out the bike stand, propped the bicycle up, and began plucking the bright, sweet flowers.

Bumblebees bud-hopped alongside Dani, but she didn't mind. There were plenty of blooms to go around and the bees didn't seem to notice her. She pulled stems and sampled nectar, one flower after the other, the sweetness dancing on her tongue. When the bees finally ventured a little too close, she stepped around to the right side of the bush to put some distance between them, and that's when she saw them: a partially obscured pair of bright white Skechers, shoved under the clumpy vine, about six inches beyond its outer edge.

*What a waste.*

Dani had been wearing her old pair of Skechers sneakers for over two years, and they were soiled beyond cleaning. She was itching for another pair, and even planned on asking for one for her birthday. The ones abandoned here were bright white and the platform version, even. They were exactly what she wanted.

*I'd kill for those. I can't believe someone just dumped them here like that.*

She was wondering whether they might be at all close to her size when it registered that the shoes weren't lying flat, but were, quite disturbingly, very, very vertical. Heels down, toes up.

As if someone was still wearing them.

Dani squatted down and pulled the vine away from the fence to get a better look. A wave of lightheadedness rippled through her as she sucked in a trembling breath.

Jennifer Cartwright lay impossibly still underneath the honeysuckle bush, the entire length of her body pressed up against the barbed wire fence so that her head, her blond hair spilled about it, was furthest in, her feet out. From the front of the bush, she had been completely hidden by the vines, but now, standing at the side with the vines pulled back, Dani could see into the less dense undergrowth and the space that held Jennifer. Her eyes raked over the girl's denim shorts and white top, both streaked with dirt, and...something else. Something the color of rust. Her skin, especially her face, bore an unnatural blue cast, as if she were cold—hypothermia-level cold—an impossibility in that unrelenting, sweltering heat.

Dani began to shake.

She knew those blue eyes well. Had seen them sparkle at school every day since they started kindergarten together. Jennifer Cartwright was vibrant, funny and kind, the sort of person who even reached out to the oddballs like Dani, despite being the most popular girl in the tenth grade at Skye High. She was beloved and lit up every room she walked into. But those eyes weren't sparkling now. All the light that had ever been in them had gone out.

From somewhere high above, a crack sounded, followed by a branch plummeting to the earth, landing with a thump nearby. Dani's heart jumped, slamming against her rib cage and solidly yanking her out of her shock-induced daze as she jumped back and screamed. Ripping her gaze away from Jennifer, Dani stumbled the few steps to her bicycle. Grasping it by the handlebars, she clumsily kicked up the stand and ran hard for several yards before finally hopping on and pedaling away as fast as her scrawny legs would allow.

It was the first time she had ever seen a dead body.

Unfortunately, it would not be the last.

## 2

---

Thirteen Years Later

There should be something terribly comforting about returning to your hometown. Something grounding and sentimental, reminding you of who you were when life started, and of all the dreams you used to have when you were still allowed to dream anything you wanted, because the truth of life and its limitations had not yet set in. But entering the streets of Skye—her old haunting grounds, her place of coming of age, her place of beginning—Dani felt none of that.

Every time she made this trip—once in mid-May to spend a week with her mom and dad, and then again at Christmas—it was the same. There was a grimness that settled over her the second she steered out of Birmingham in the boring rental they would give her at the airport, headed for the little town of Skye in the western part of Central Alabama. She would navigate through "Malfunction Junction" at the north end of Birmingham and take I-20 west to Tuscaloosa, trees and brush and flat fields of corn or cotton or other crops, scrolling by until she reached Highway 82. Then she would veer south, her apprehension mounting until finally turning onto the main road leading into Skye. That's when the vivid memories of Jennifer Cartwright would hit hard.

Fortunately, though the memories always lingered in the background, their intensity didn't last long after arriving, as she was always soon consumed with her mom and dad and their situation—meals, chores too taxing for them, and doctor visits —and catching up with friends she hadn't seen in half a year. There were only two she kept up with: Peter Welling and Sasha Mason, the same two friends she had been planning to meet on *that* day. They had managed to maintain a close relationship since graduating ten years before, even though she had ended up on the other side of the universe at Boston College, while they, like so many of their classmates, had stayed home and joined the ranks of the Alabama Crimson Tide.

Most high school friends lose touch over time. That wasn't their story. Before she had left for college, Sasha and Peter were the two people who knew her best, and even after all this time, they still were. They knew her better than her parents. Better than her older sister, Nikki, who had landed in San Diego and hadn't made it home to Skye one time in the last three years before this past March. And even better than Dr. Joline, the therapist she had been seeing in Boston for the last ten years, who knew every secret Dani had ever had.

Sasha and Peter were special. Her anchors. And she was theirs. So they promised to make the distance work, and they did, with phone calls and emails and Dani's visits to Skye— even after Dani permanently moved to Boston after college. Even after Sasha got married, and Dani got married, and Peter got married, and Dani got divorced.

The lynchpin of the relationship, they all knew, was that

they still saw each other twice a year, when Dani would come home. It made sense that she was the one that traveled to them. Since Dani's parents still lived in Skye, she needed to come home anyway. Especially since Nikki rarely did, instead flying her parents out to see her and her kids. So, Dani always made her regularly scheduled trips home. But this year was different. For a lot of reasons, not the least of which was that this year, she was home in *July*.

July in Skye.

By design, she hadn't been home during July since graduating from college, after which she no longer had to spend summers there. Dani didn't like being in town during the summer months for obvious reasons, or at least it was obvious to Dr. Joline. But this time, she hadn't had the luxury of choosing to avoid it. So here she was, rolling into town, cruising over the Claythorne River bridge and braking at the red light.

Her parents' street was just ahead on the right. Applegate Lane. 1108 Applegate Lane. Allen and Marie's home for the last thirty years. The only home Dani had ever known outside of Boston. Normally, she would be going straight there to see them first. To settle in. To bring her bags to her old room, wallpapered with pale-pink posies and grey shag carpet, sit at their memory-soaked kitchen table—home of ten thousand family dinners—and have a cup of fresh ground coffee far too late in the afternoon to allow for a good night's sleep. But when the light turned green, she drove through the intersection, passed by the street and continued on toward the center of town, sadness squeezing her heart like a vise.

This was not a normal trip.

*I'll never have a normal trip here again. Whatever "normal" was.*

Brushing away a tear, she turned her thoughts to Green's Drugs where, with any luck, Sasha and Peter were already waiting for her. She rolled down Main Street, the well-kept line of two-story brick buildings on either side still resembling something out of Mayberry: Glenda's Gift Shop on the corner; Perry & Pear Men's Clothiers on her right, and beside it Hinkle's Toys and Books. And just beyond that, Green's Drugs.

A welcome lightness seeped through the sadness, spreading into the corners of her as she imagined it—the long, melamine counter, with its high stools and chipped edges, where they would order root beer floats and cheeseburgers, and laugh and catch up, and maybe, just maybe, for a precious little while, she might be able to pretend that nothing was different at all.

NOT SURPRISINGLY, Green's Drugs was packed, as usual. Every seat in the place was taken—every single one at the long counter and tables—the space noisy with chatter and thick with the smell of grilled ground beef and grease. A few years ago, when the AllMart had opened up just half a mile away, it had killed off Green's drugstore business. But the soda counter was so popular that the owner had given it one last go, converting it into a full service diner. The gamble had worked and, so now, though they couldn't buy hairspray there any longer, they *were* able to order amazing cheeseburgers and fries to go with their milkshakes. Keeping the name "Green's Drugs" often proved confusing to town visitors, but the locals loved it. And it made it easy to tell who the outsiders were—anyone who came in asking where they could find the painkillers was clearly only passing through town.

Dani, Peter and Sasha sat on three adjacent, black-pleather stools at the end of the white counter farthest from the front door. Dani sat between the other two, all of them hunched over their food, sucking down milkshakes as they talked and laughed.

"...and then, five hours later, I finally found them. *In the kids' toilet.* Trent said he decided my keys needed to 'go potty,'" Sasha said, putting a hand to her brow and shaking her head. "Do you believe that? My keys? I mean, why?"

Dani had seen Sasha perform that little gesture of frustration a million times during their decades of friendship. She felt a smile blossom at the familiarity as she dipped a fry in ketchup, stuffed it in her mouth and nodded, continuing to listen as Sasha shared her woeful tales of chasing after her two young children. Despite the exhaustion Sasha claimed to experience daily at the hands of her little ones, she was as beautiful and vibrant as ever, with her flawless deep-brown skin and shiny black hair in tight ringlets that framed her face before extending nearly a full foot below her shoulders. Almost as if it were a scripted joke, at that moment Dani looked up from her plate, her gaze passing across her own reflection in the mirrored wall behind the counter.

*I look tired.*

Tired, but not terrible, really. Just a bit...rumply. Her bright blond-treated hair, wavy and dropping to just beneath her shoulders, had flyaways poking out here and there. The oversized short-sleeved shirt she wore over cropped yoga pants was wrinkled after two hours of flying from Boston to D.C., a two-hour layover there, followed by another two-hour flight to Birmingham and the hour-and-a-half drive from the airport to Skye. And there were the beginnings of black mascara smudges beneath her brown eyes. She ran a hand over herself, smoothing her hair, straightening wrinkles and rubbing away the mascara smudges, although she couldn't do anything about the faint circles their removal revealed.

Peter shook a finger at Sasha. "That boy is gonna be trouble. You're gonna have to be tougher on him," he said, before taking a huge bite of cheeseburger.

"Yeah, you say that now, but just wait," Sasha said, a knowing smirk on her face. "When that baby comes next month, you'll be singing a different tune. You'll get one look at her and be putty in her hands. It'll be 'anything you want, baby.'"

Peter shook his head in protest, but Dani nodded. "She's got you there," she agreed, then licked the salt from the fries off her finger. It wasn't ladylike, but she did it anyway. Ladylike wasn't really her style.

"You both sound like Amy," Peter said. "She's afraid she'll have to be the bad cop of our parenting duo."

Ten years after graduation, Peter still looked like a kid to Dani, dressed in a white polo shirt and khaki shorts, not a face wrinkle in sight, his shaggy brown hair ending in big curls at his ears and neck. Maybe it was working with kids as the director of the town's Recreation and Youth Center that kept him looking young. Whatever it was, she wished she had it. She had found two grey hairs last month hiding amongst her subtle blond-highlights, prompting the more thorough, full-on blond dye job she now sported.

"Well, if your wife needs any help figuring out how to play bad cop, have her call me," Dani said, as the bell suspended over the front door jingled. Out of habit and training, she instinctively glanced over. A couple of teenagers slid inside, looking for a seat.

"What would you know about it?" Peter said, baiting her with his tone. "You've only been a detective for two months."

"Maybe, but I've been a cop for six years and the good-cop-bad-cop routine is the first thing they teach you in the academy."

"Like they would have to teach you that," Sasha said, rolling her eyes.

"What's that supposed to mean?" Dani asked, doing her best to look legitimately offended, but knowing exactly where Sasha was headed. She didn't mind. The banter was one of her favorite things about coming home to see them. It was what made this home.

"Please. In a room full of people, you're going to be the one looking to start something," Sasha pressed.

"Um, are you saying I'm antagonistic?" Dani said, working hard not to laugh, all too aware of her long-standing tendency to stir the pot whenever possible.

"Um, I'm saying you're a troublemaker," Sasha replied.

Dani fixed her face in mock outrage. "I don't think *that's* fair—"

"I'll bet the Andrews twins didn't think it was fair that you announced in pre-cal that one of them had been seeing the other's boyfriend, *with them both in the room,*" Sasha said, looking as if she had just played the high trump card in a game of spades.

Dani pursed her lips. "Well," she recovered, shrugging, "the truth needed to come out somehow—"

"So," Peter boomed, causing Dani and Sasha's heads to swivel toward him. "Subject change," he said, his tone softening as he eyed Dani intently. "Have you been to the house yet?"

The lightness of the easy banter of a moment ago evaporated as a weight thudded to the floor of Dani's chest. "No," she answered, then sighed impatiently. "Could we just not talk about this right now? Okay? Not yet. Tell me more about what's been going on with you two—"

"It's just, we've been here for half an hour," Peter said, "and other than telling us that you're okay and you don't want to talk about it—"

"That's because I *don't* want to talk about it, all right? Not now. I just wanted...a little normalcy first," Dani said.

"Sure," Peter relented. "Whatever you need. I just want you to know that if we can do anything, if you want help sorting through things or packing up—"

Sasha reached across Dani to cover Peter's hand with her own, gently squeezing it where it rested on the counter. He fell silent. "She gets it, Peter. She knows we're here for her if she needs help. Don't you, Dani?"

Dani nodded. "I do. Honestly, I'm fine. It's something I need to do by myself, I think."

"But," Sasha started, "when it's box-moving time—"

"You'll be the first one I'll call."

"No, *he's* the first one you call for the heavy lifting," Sasha said, pointing a finger at Peter. "I'm an excellent supervisor, though."

Dani chuckled. "Right. Speaking of supervising, how's the reunion coming?"

Sasha straightened up proudly. "The Skye High Class of 1998 Reunion is nearly all set," she said, rubbing her hands together.

"Which means it's nowhere near done," Peter dead-panned.

Sasha's eyes flashed, an aggrieved expression washing over her face. "I *know* you didn't just say that."

"You planned my wedding reception, remember?" he said, his brows rising. "I have two words for you—no shrimp."

"How many times do I have to tell you, it's not my fault the caterer didn't check her email—"

"Soooo," Dani drawled, holding the o's out until the other two had stopped chattering, "what I want to know is how you got roped into heading this up, Sash?"

The bell at the door jingled again and, again, Dani automatically glanced over. *Single adult male. Over 6 foot. Very dark hair, almost black, cut short, tips curling at the ends, dark eyes, slight five o'clock shadow. Sweaty T-shirt and running shorts. Handsome—Stop,* she finally told herself, giving her head a little shake. *You're not on duty.* But before she turned away, the man caught her looking and smiled amusedly as Dani broke the connection, feeling her face turn hot. Clocking "handsome" as an identifying characteristic of an individual was a bit of a stretch for a standard rundown, but hey, she was human, wasn't she? Still, she felt...busted. Shoving down the lingering flickers of embarrassment, she returned her full attention to Sasha.

"...and the class president always gets the honor," Sasha said, spreading her hands wide and grinning, her white teeth gleaming. "So it fell to me."

"Don't worry, Dani, she's been spreading the love," Peter said wryly. "I don't know if she's told you, but you're down for the decorating committee. And you got your director of music right here," he said, patting his chest. "Picked the band, the set list, the song for the memorial—"

At the word, "memorial," Dani's nerves fired, as if she had plunged a finger into a socket. "What memorial?" she asked, and in the mirror behind the counter, she watched Peter's gaze cut sharply to Sasha before shooting quickly down to the countertop, where it remained. An undercurrent of tension prickled the hairs on Dani's skin.

*They're holding something back.*

"We didn't want to say anything before now," Sasha finally said after several silent moments. "We thought if you knew, you might not come."

"What memorial?" Dani repeated, though she thought that she already knew the answer.

Sasha sighed. "Jennifer Cartwright's." She twisted in her seat toward Dani, her body curving slightly, almost as if trying to draw Dani into her thinking. "She would have graduated with us. A lot of people have asked whether we're doing something to honor her, and it just felt wrong not to acknowledge her somehow. I'm sorry I didn't warn you, I just know how sensitive you are when it comes to her—"

"No, it's fine. I get it," Dani said, and forced a small smile that she did not feel to prove it. "It's a nice idea. She deserves that."

*I just wish you'd told me. So I could prepare myself.*

"It will be nice, I promise. Not overdramatic or long or

anything. So...you'll still come, right?" There was a note of pleading in Sasha's voice and the concern lining her eyes made it clear she was truly worried that Dani would find the memorial a deal-breaker and blow off the reunion altogether.

"Of course, I'll come."

"And decorate?"

Dani narrowed her eyes playfully. "And decorate," she said grudgingly, pushing her plate, with its two remaining fries, away from her. As long as she left a couple on the plate, and a sip or two in the milkshake glass, she could feel like she hadn't *completely* cheated on her resolution to eat cleaner this year. She lazily ran a finger around the edge of the glass, aware that the conversation had taken a turn that gave her the opening to bring it up, but dreading it all the same. Finally, her finger dropped from the glass and she dove in. "So, since we're on Jennifer...I think I'm going to visit him."

Peter squinted, a small hiss of air escaping his lips. "You just saw him in March. I thought you were done with that."

"Last time you said it was too hard," Sasha added.

Dani picked up the wrapper from her straw and began playing with it, folding it in half, and then in half again, and again. "You know no one else visits him from here?" she asked, her focus still on the wrapper.

"Yeah, we know. You've told us," Peter said.

"So, I'll bet he hasn't had a visitor since me."

"He's a convicted murderer," Sasha said. "And—" she reached out to squeeze Dani's arm just as Dani opened her mouth to speak, "before you start in, I *know* you think he's innocent—"

"He *is* innocent," Dani protested.

Sasha offered a thin smile, ripe with understanding. "We go through this every time you visit. I know you *believe* he's innocent, but no one else does. And you can't prove it. No one here wants anything to do with the man that killed Jennifer. It's a chapter they want to keep closed."

"They didn't know him the way I do. The way I did. He didn't kill her and he's been sitting in that prison, rotting, for thirteen years."

"Every time you go, you just rip the wound open," Peter said. "Last time you told us to remind you why you shouldn't go back. So, we're reminding you."

"Well, I was wrong. I'm not ripping a wound open, because it never healed in the first place, because they never found her killer. I found her. And I couldn't help them. I couldn't give them anything that led to real answers. So, they put the wrong person away because it was easy, and it's haunted me for nearly half my life. The least I can do is visit him. It's thirty minutes. I think I can spare it."

Silence fell between them, as Sasha and Peter shifted uncomfortably in tandem. Dani understood. Really, she did. They went through this every time she came back down here. They had to be tired of it by now. After every visit she would tell them to remind her why she shouldn't go see him on the next trip down, because it was just *so* hard and dragged up so many demons. But then months would pass in Boston, and the guilt would set in and the obsession would gnaw at her, hungry for attention and the injustice would cry out to be undone...

"It's just...we worry about you, Dani," Peter said, his eyes soft. "Not letting this go. It's like the cop in you can't accept that there isn't a mystery to be solved here. I don't know, it won't let you...move on. It won't let you rest."

"I live in Massachusetts. I think I've managed to move on."

"You know what I'm saying." His words were pregnant with meaning, conveying the history, care and concern borne of a two-decade friendship. The smile that curved his mouth was kind but sad, and Dani's love for this sweet man, this unwavering friend, overtook her. She wanted to throw her arms around him, wanted to say "thank you for loving me so well, Peter," right there in the diner. But instead, she lightly bumped her shoulder against his.

"Yeah, I do," she said. "But, I'm fine." When the doubt creasing her friends' visages failed to dissipate, Dani widened her eyes, letting an exasperated chuckle escape. "I'm serious, guys. I'm fine. Okay?"

In a way that seemed to Dani more like surrender than actual belief, Sasha and Peter exchanged a knowing look, then exhaled, their postures easing.

*I'll take it,* she thought. "Good," Dani said. "Besides, we've got more important things to discuss, like," she turned her gaze to Sasha, "why in the world you would put *me* on the decorating committee when you know good and well my idea of decorating my apartment involved throwing a blanket over a pull-out sofa I found on the street and hanging a plastic-framed poster of George Costanza over it?"

They stayed there for another hour, rehashing old, funny stories and sharing all the new ones. But as she listened, with a perfectly content and well-adjusted expression appropriately pinned to her face, all Dani could think about was the new loss that awaited her when she left there, and the old loss that, no matter what she had told her friends, was compelling her to rip the stitches from her poorly patched-up veins and bleed out all over again, a guilt payment to the ghosts of her past.

## 3
———

Dani allowed herself one last heaving sob, blew her nose again, and inhaled a broken breath. Leaning her elbows on the old kitchen table, she rubbed her hands hard across her cheeks, then over her head, whisking the better part of the tears away.

All it had taken was one cup of coffee. One stupid cup of coffee. She had been fine when she walked into her parents' kitchen through the door that led in from the garage. She was fine when she flipped on the light and dropped her stuff right at the door, the loud thud sounding incredibly hollow in the uninhabited house. But very quickly a weariness had set in as she looked around at it all—all her parents' things, their whole lives sitting there in the quiet. In the dark, with no one left to own them. *I'll make a cup of coffee,* she had thought, *and just sit and breathe for a minute. That'll help.*

It hadn't.

She and Nikki had cleared out the perishables back in March, in the days following the funeral. But that was as far as they had gotten. Neither of them had had it in them to do more.

So now, two months after the estate had closed, it was all still there as if Allen and Marie Lake had only just driven to church or dinner or something. All of it. Including her father's coffee beans.

Dani knew exactly where to find the grinder. Second cabinet to the left of the sink. Her dad didn't—hadn't—believed in buying pre-ground. The panic-inducing, sudden sound of coffee beans becoming gritty dust at six in the morning had essentially been her alarm clock for the eighteen years she had lived at home. The tightly sealed bag of beans—a dark roast from Hawaii, one of her dad's favorites—was predictably waiting in the cabinet just above the coffee maker. But as she ground the beans, rather than making her feel better, Dani sensed the wetness beginning to gather at the corners of her eyes, then forming drops as she poured the water in the coffee maker and finally, cascading down her cheeks as she stood at the counter, waiting as the pot brewed.

*Drip. Drip. Drip.*

Tears and percolating coffee fell in partnership as such overwhelming sadness overtook her, exacerbated by growing anxiety as her brain scrolled through all the things—so, so many things—that had to be done before she returned to Boston in one week. Her shoulders now shaking as muffled sobs racked her, she shuffled over to the shelf on the wall opposite and selected a mug from her mother's collection—a pink one emblazoned with the words "Do not speak to me until this cup is empty." Zombie-like, Dani poured the strong, full-bodied brew into the mug, so distracted that it nearly overflowed before she righted the pot at the last second, barely avoiding scalding herself. She returned to her chair at the table and sat down, took one sip which burned her lip, and burst into a torrent of weeping.

That was two hours ago. Two hours of crying uncontrollably as the coffee grew cool, then cold, every memory ever contained in that house breaking over her, ripping her heart to shreds, the raw pain of it as strong and cruel as if she had only just learned that her parents had died. As if that news hadn't been delivered four months earlier, in a late-night call from Nikki while Dani was working her way out of a laboratory-themed escape room on a rare girls-night-out in Boston.

Two hours. But slowly, very slowly, the intensity diminished. The sobbing turned to sniffling. The desperate grief to exhaustion.

*Enough.*

Rubbing her red-raw eyes and dragging a sleeve across her nose, Dani stood. She lifted the cold, still-full cup of coffee, and dumped it into the sink.

*I need to get out of here.*

Without a plan, without any notion of where she was headed, Dani strode to the door leading to the garage and walked out, pulling it shut behind her with a gentle click.

*Now what?*

Dani's mind was numb, and she intentionally fought to keep from thinking about anything at all as her feet kept going, out of the garage, down the drive and turning right down her old block. She had done far too much thinking in the last hours. Step after step she continued down the asphalt, the same street on which she had ridden that old yellow-and-pea-green bicycle thousands of times.

She passed one house and then another. The way was so familiar that it was easy to not think and to just...go. None of it was new. It was all so unchanged. Nothing to notice, nothing to process, for which her spent mind was grateful. She was beginning to really feel the exhaustion though, a dull ache starting to whisper in her joints and feet after this very, very long day. But she didn't want to stop. She didn't want to go back. Not yet.

The glowing tangerine sun had finally set, leaving behind a dusky twilight soundtracked by a rising chorus of cicadas. They called to Dani, beckoning her to continue, and she did. Until she finally came to it.

Of course she had known it was coming. But it made her breath catch in her chest all the same: that pathway, that cut-through between the two houses that would take her to Dr. Beecher's property if she went past the line of pine trees that formed the border of their backyards.

Inexplicably, her feet turned toward it, and she felt almost disembodied, as if she were watching someone else's feet walking in that direction, and then between the houses, through the backyards and farther, until she found herself leaning against the long white fence of Smith and Wesson's old pasture.

*What am I doing?*

The horses were, of course, gone. Thirteen years was a long time. Still, she closed her eyes, imagining them and how they had looked that day, ignoring her clicking tongue as she beckoned to them beneath the blazing sun. Right before everything changed forever.

*Why am I here?*

She had never come back after finding Jennifer. Not once. Any time the thought of returning occurred to her, it would make her insides writhe, even as a grown woman sitting on her lumpy second-hand couch in her tiny Boston apartment, thousands of miles away from that riverbank. But here she was, as close to this place as she had ever been since that day, still cresting the waves of the emotional storm she had just ridden out in her parents' kitchen, and oddly, the thing that began to fill her...was calm.

Dani's eyes flicked open at the surprise of that realization, and suddenly she *knew* that she needed to do this, needed to face it. Forcing her feet to move, she started down the dirt path between the pasture on the left and the field on the right. Unlike that day in 1995, no corn stalks grew there now. The field was empty, just raw unused reddish dirt. She had heard that, at some point, the rear property had been divided from the main estate and sold to Mr. and Mrs. Pitts, the caretakers that used to farm that field for Dr. Beecher. She wondered if they still lived in the small house set way back at the southern edge of the property, or if they, like Smith and Wesson, were long gone too.

Her feet left the dirt path, striking the gravel drive that ran perpendicular to it, which, if she followed it all the way to the left, would lead her to the main road. But she wasn't headed to the main road today. Instead, the rocks crunched against the soles of her sandals as she crossed the drive, headed for the riverbank beyond. The second, the very second, she lifted a foot from the last of the gravel and placed it on the uneven grassy earth, a low vibration began humming within her, spreading from her chest, to her jaw, then her fingers and toes. She was close. So close. And her body knew it.

To this point, she had avoided looking to the right, instead keeping her focus straight ahead, in line with the dirt path. But now, with nowhere else to go, she slowly swiveled her gaze in that direction.

It was still there.

The honeysuckle vine with its yellow and white and green billowing over the barbed-wire fence was still there. She hadn't been sure it would be, because the summer after she found Jennifer, someone ripped the vine out—cut it from the fence, chopped it at the roots and pulled it up, leaving gaping holes in the earth. She hadn't seen it for herself, of course, but not unexpectedly, the place was notorious among her classmates—visited on tacky dares and such—and word about the bush's demise had gotten out.

*They must have missed some roots,* she thought, because now it was back, more massive than before, easily stretching thirty feet down the old, rusty wire fence. It was so wide now that she didn't need to step as far down to the right to reach it. Now, just ten quick steps and she was there.

She reached a hand out, almost as if expecting something to jump out and bite her. But it was leafy and soft, the pistils of the flowers and their bulbous tips tickling her palm as she passed her hand over them. A bird somewhere near the river cawed, drawing Dani's eyes up and over the water. This summer had seen an uncharacteristic amount of rain, and the river was midway up the bank, rushing and gurgling. Dani's gaze drifted back to the honeysuckle as she gauged her position.

*This isn't where I found her. She was much farther down to the right.*

The steady vibration in Dani's body accelerated as she left that spot and drifted closer to where she thought she had first seen Jennifer's Skechers. A buzzing crescendoed in her ears as she stepped nearer and nearer, until—

*This is it. She was somewhere...right about...here.*

An overwhelming sense of standing on holy ground overtook her, something akin to reverence, and she became acutely aware of her heart thumping in her ears. She breathed in deeply through her nose for four counts, held it for four more, then exhaled through her mouth for another four. Breathe in. Hold. Breathe out.

*Calm. Down.*

Another bird cawed in the growing darkness. She stood there, waiting for...well, she wasn't sure what. Just...something. But there wasn't anything, because this was just a place where nothing had happened for a very long time. It was just darkness and space and earth and sky and harmless honeysuckle. Nothing more.

*You are such an idiot.*

Why she was standing there, in the place that had haunted her for thirteen years instead of back home, sitting at their kitchen table, drinking coffee and planning how to sort and clear out all her parents' belongings so they could finally sell the house? What was she doing chasing ghosts where none existed?

*Maybe, because now, home haunts you more than this place does.*

The instant the words passed through her brain, she rejected them. As usual she was overthinking. She was upset and wasn't processing well, and somehow, this temporary emotional breakdown or departure from sanity or, whatever, had brought her here. A place she had absolutely no business being. Feeling a clarity she hadn't possessed since first walking into her parents' kitchen, she resolutely turned to go—when, somewhere farther down to the right, along the riverbank, a flash of something barely visible in the last vestiges of dusk crossed her view.

*The old shed.*

It had been there for decades, a small structure that couldn't have been more than a dozen feet deep and wide at most, set against the barbed-wire fence, close to the edge of the riverbank. Though the shed had belonged to Dr. Beecher, it was nearer the caretakers' field and they had used it to store equipment—a mower, garden tools, tiller, and such—keeping these things conveniently close to the fields and out of the weather.

Darkness was falling quickly now, and it was difficult to see the structure well from that distance. But Dani recalled that dark rustic wood formed its simple, thin walls, and that the roof had been made of sheets of shiny ribbed aluminum. There was a time in her early childhood, long before finding Jennifer, that Dani had regularly used the shed as a hiding place when playing hide-and-seek with some of the neighborhood kids.

*What was it like now?*

Curiosity, and perhaps a need to connect with a time before it all went so wrong, caused her to abandon her decision to head home. Instead she walked the twenty-five or so yards to the shed. It had not held up well over the years. The weathered, grimy wood slats had rotted in places. The sheets of aluminum, which formed a slight peak at the roof's center, had suffered significant corrosion, and were now riddled with sporadic holes and sharp rusty edges.

It still sat on concrete blocks, protecting the interior and its contents from direct contact with the earth and its destructive moisture. Once upon a time, a short wooden ramp had led up to the door, allowing for the wheeled machinery to be rolled inside. But the ramp was gone, leaving a significant gap between the ground and the door's threshold. Dani grasped the door's handle and pulled, the heavy, slatted piece creaking and testing the strength of its hinges as it swung outward.

It was quiet and forbiddingly dark inside, with only the minimal light of the rising moon filtering in through the holes in the wood and metal. Dani took her phone out and opened it, using the light from the screen as a makeshift flashlight. Holding it before her, she hiked one foot up onto the raised floor, then, bracing a hand on the door frame, pulled herself up the rest of the way and stepped inside.

All the tools and equipment were gone. The only thing stored here now were spiders and, disturbingly, more than one discarded, translucent snake skin. A bird's nest with grass, twigs and what looked like a strand of colored twine was tucked high into one of the corners where the walls met the aluminum roofline. The wooden plank floor was covered with dust and dirt, animal droppings and tracks, and chipped bark and leaves that had either blown in through one of the holes or had been dragged inside by some critter.

She turned to face the far left corner. This was the spot where she had hunkered down whenever she used the shed as a hiding place. Back then, a riding mower was parked directly in front of that corner and had served as great cover. Shining the light in that direction, she stepped into that space, almost feeling like her eight-year-old self. She turned again, facing out, then crouched down and imagined the mower there in front of her as she would peek around its side...

*Footprints.*

The gleam from her phone had fallen across the floor planks between her and the door, revealing a number of distinct footprints in the thick dust and dirt. Human footprints. A chill fluttered through her. Some were hers, but others weren't. They were from larger shoes, man-sized, she thought. And they did not all bear the same pattern. These were from multiple visits. But how long ago? Recently or months or years earlier?

And why? Why would any adult male come here—more than once?

*Why would you?*

Maybe it was someone like her, tapping into some sentimental memory. But, no, the more obvious explanation was a vagrant—someone who had used the shed as shelter. But then she would expect cans or wrappers or newspapers or something to indicate someone had stayed there. There was none of that. And a vagrant with multiple pairs of shoes?

Dani traced the footprints with the light. They seemed to congregate around one particular plank a few feet in front of her. This plank was somewhat cleaner than the rest. Covered in much less dirt and dust and, in fact, it appeared the residue had been brushed across its surface, in a swiping motion if she wasn't mistaken. Possibly in an attempt to clean it, although, the amount left behind suggested that someone might have actually been attempting to *replace* the debris. To make it appear undisturbed.

Dani knelt down, bending over the plank. She pressed a hand on one end.

It moved.

Though nails still secured it to the crossbeam beneath, there was a lot of give. Movement that suggested the plank was only marginally secured. Easy to remove. She aimed the light into the gap between the floorboards and her breathing stuttered.

There was something under there.

Setting down her phone, Dani crammed her fingers against the small gap where the head of the loose plank met the next one. It was narrow, maybe only a quarter-inch wide, but it was enough for her fingernails to get a hold. She ripped upward with more power than was necessary and the board flew up, slamming against the wall. Dani rocked back on her heels as the board dropped to the floor with a bang, then rattled to silence. Leaning forward, Dani peered into the space beneath. There on the dirt floor was a thick, black plastic bag, wrapped in several tight passes around whatever was inside it, tied shut with brown twine.

Her pulse racing, Dani snatched the bag out of its hiding place, unknotted the twine and unraveled the bag from around its contents. Wary of what might be inside—needles were always a possibility—she dumped the contents onto the floor.

A single book slid out, hitting the floor with a thunk. It was pastel pink with a rainbow spanning the cover, and beneath it the words "My Diary" printed in glittery, gold letters. Dani reached one hand out, opened the cover to the first page and screamed.

SHE HAD SCREAMED. Definitely screamed, and his insides plunged because he thought he knew what that meant. Then suddenly she flew out of the shed, running like a madwoman being chased, tearing across the gravel road, then back down the dirt path toward the neighborhood street that lay beyond. Though he couldn't hear anything from this distance, given the way she was shaking and running so awkwardly, he suspected she was crying, or maybe something more violent than that—sobbing—but it was hard to tell. It was so dark and she was running so fast.

He had worried about her finding it the minute he had seen her step inside. Because if anyone was going to find it, she would. She had almost as much of a connection as he did. In fact, on some level, he *wanted* her to find it. He had watched as the light she was using inside the shed—probably from her phone—pierced the holes in the shed's walls, cutting into the darkness outside and meeting his gaze where he hid on the riverbank, watching. Then there was banging and rattling and, a minute later, her desperate scream, and he knew with certainty that she *had* discovered it.

She had nearly tripped over the door's threshold in her frantic escape, clumsily dropping the one foot distance to the ground below, carrying the treasure in her arms, clutching it to her chest as if protecting it from any unseen dangers that might threaten to take it from her. Because she knew it was special too. She, of all people, understood its sanctity and what it represented.

His gaze tracked her until her form disappeared behind the line of pine trees bordering the backyards of the adjacent neighborhood. Then he turned away, his mind spinning as he stole back down the riverbank, planning his next move.

FLUSHED and her heart still pounding, Dani sat at her kitchen table, her hands sheathed in her mother's purple dishwashing gloves, holding the cover of the diary open with one hand, while caressing its inscription with the other. The shock that had seized her upon reading those words on the floor of that dirty old shed still gripped her, leaving her mind fuzzy, her thoughts disjointed. The second she had read that page, time had stopped, and all in the world had fallen away, except this one thing.

*This Diary Belongs To:*
*Jennifer Cartwright*

In the moments after finding the diary, she had remained bent over on the shed's floor, cradling the book in her hands, frantic over what to do. Those uncertain seconds had seemed to last forever, but in reality couldn't have been more than a minute, as she debated what to do.

*Did I make the right decision?*

The thought of staying there, on that dank, musty floor, waiting for someone to arrive, safeguarding the...evidence... until the blue lights made their way up the gravel drive and finally flooded the shed, had made her skin crawl. Finding Jennifer's diary there, in that shallow grave, in that abandoned tomb of a building, was like finding her body all over again, hidden beneath the twisted vines....no. No. She couldn't have stayed there another minute. She had needed to be gone from that place.

But she couldn't just leave the diary in the shed. What if something happened to it before the police got back there? Then again, taking it was essentially disturbing the evidence, compromising it on some level, no matter what precautions she took. Procedure dictated that the instant she had realized what she had, the second she had seen Jennifer's name, she should have dropped the diary back in the bag and called the Chief. Then she should have stayed, securing the scene until the investigating officer arrived.

Her shell-shocked mind had waffled back and forth, until, finally, the overwhelming need to just *not* be there won out, as did the training that told her leaving the evidence unprotected was not an acceptable option. So, she had wrapped it back up in its plastic bag and run home.

Dani let go of the book with one hand to take a sip from the glass of ice water she had poured herself. The liquid rolled down her throat, the sharp cold sobering her thinking a bit. Hoping to continue clearing the fog, she gulped down more, still staring at the diary's "Belongs To" page and Jennifer's name written in hot-pink, bubbly cursive.

She knew she should call the Chief now. She had no excuse. She was home. She was safe. The diary was safe. She should call the Chief so that he could send someone over who would enact the proper protocols and preserve the chain of evidence. She knew this. She was a good cop.

But she was also a person who had been haunted by the murdered owner of this diary every day for the last thirteen years. A person obsessed with the knowledge that the wrong man had been convicted of that murder—a good man, an innocent man—and that no one believed it but her. After all these years, after so many dead ends and unanswered questions, she held something in her hands that might finally be able to shed light on the truth.

And that was why she did not call the Chief. It was also why, though every cell of Dani's being screamed at her to start reading already, to turn to the next page, she had not been able to do so. Because as much as she wanted to know, to understand, to find answers—once she turned the pages, there would be no unlearning the private thoughts and dreams, the memories and secrets, that had been laid bare on them. What if the truths scrawled inside weren't the truths she had so desperately sought all these years?

*But, I have to know.*

And so, her mind reeling with all the excuses she would spout to the Chief in the morning to explain her lapse in professional judgment, she resolutely turned the page.

# 4

The first thing Dani did was flip through the pages quickly, scanning to get an overall sense of what was contained inside. The entries began with January 1, 1995, and went all the way through July 8, 1995, the day before Dani found Jennifer. She was apparently religious about writing in it, because it didn't look like she had missed a single day. The entries were all long, at least one page each, though usually more. A record of every day of the final year that she had lived. Which meant there were 193 entries to get through.

*But what about at the end? Maybe there's something in her last days that might give the murderer away? Could it be that simple?*

That possibility thrilling her, Dani split the book down the middle, found the last entry for July 8, and started reading the precious, perfect, last recorded words of a girl that would be dead by the next day.

But there was no smoking gun. No name scribbled in ink descending down the page, identifying Jennifer's killer. No, it was just...about a lot of nothing. She wrote about the heat and how she hated how it made her sweat, and the purple thistles she had seen on the roadside and stopped to pick, and plans with her best friend, Kendall, to go to the movies that weekend. All standard teenage stuff.

Until the third paragraph, and these words sent a jolt through Dani's heart. Because Jennifer Cartwright had written about the fight she was still having with her boyfriend.

*Boyfriend?*

As far as Dani knew, Jennifer Cartwright had not been dating anyone at the time of her death. Of course, it was possible Dani wouldn't have known about it—they weren't close, after all—but someone, at the very least Jennifer's best friend Kendall, would have known. And then, it would have come out during the investigation because Kendall would have told the police. Unless Jennifer had kept his existence a secret from Kendall too. But why would Jennifer have done that?

*A boyfriend. She had a secret boyfriend. Which means there was another potential suspect.*

Excitement bubbled in Dani as, hoping for clarification, she flipped backward through several entries—July 7, July 6, July 5 —scrutinizing each one. The entries consisted of multiple pages, and while they mentioned that Jennifer and her boyfriend were fighting, other than saying it was related to something they were keeping from people and how she was making him feel badly about himself, she didn't provide helpful details.

The next entry, July 4, was completely useless. There was nothing about the boyfriend at all. Instead it offered a lengthy description of a party at the lake at Jennifer's cousin's house, including details ranging from who was there to what they ate to who stayed up the longest on the wakeboard.

Dani realized that reading the entries in reverse order wasn't going to work. Yes, it had let Dani confirm that Jennifer hadn't identified the killer in the days leading up to her death, and it had revealed a mysterious, unnamed boyfriend, which was very promising. But Dani could waste a lot of time reading it backward, hoping to stumble on the right entry and, what's more, hoping that she would understand it completely once she did. But to really understand what had happened, and to be sure to not miss a single relevant tidbit or nuance, she would need to read every entry in order. It would be slower and excruciatingly suspenseful, but there was no way around it. Otherwise she would risk accidentally missing something important because she didn't understand the context. How would Dani know what was important, unless she started at the beginning?

Settling in for a long night, Dani hunched over in her kitchen chair, turned back to the beginning of the diary and started reading.

She didn't get very far.

After wading through just half of January 1995, her lower back started really aching, so at ten thirty she moved from the kitchen table to the couch to get a bit more comfortable. She propped a pillow behind her head and one behind her lumbar region and read on. The third week of January was mostly consumed with details about the new Jetta Jennifer's father promised to buy her on her sixteenth birthday in August, an ongoing fight with her friend Kendall over a boy Jennifer didn't think Kendall should be dating, and Jennifer's obsession with the shows *Beverly Hills 90210* and *Party of Five*.

*Party of Five.*

That was a throwback. Dani had loved the show too. She closed her eyes, grasping for the names of the male leads, both of whom she'd had a crush on. The next thing she knew, she was waking up at seven a.m. on the same couch, make-up smeared, hair askew, with the diary laying open on her chest.

Now, two hours later, Dani sat behind the wheel of her rental car, parked in the second row of the lot of the main—and only—precinct of the Skye Police Department, sipping coffee from a travel mug emblazoned with "First Bank of Skye," that she had borrowed from her parents' cupboard. She had finally managed to grind, brew *and* drink her father's coffee without shedding a single tear, so, hopefully, she was starting to get a grip on herself.

As she swallowed, she relished the heat that spread through her. She held the mug, waiting for the caffeine to kick in and energize her mucky brain as she stared through her windshield at the long, rectangular brick building with its sculpted steel letters posted above the door identifying it as the police station. She had been sitting there like that for fifteen minutes trying to decide what to do, or rather, *how* to do what she came to do. It wasn't just energy she needed. A bit of courage would come in handy too. Glancing over at the passenger seat, a mass of guilty knots twisting her gut, she eyed Jennifer's diary, cocooned in the plastic bag Dani had found it in, all tucked protectively inside a large, clear zip-top bag.

*Maybe I could just run in, drop it off at the front desk with a note and run out.*

As if that would ever work. The Chief knew where to find her. Had known since the day she was born. There was no way around it. She was going to take a licking, and that was all there was to it, but the longer she waited, the worse it would be. Depositing the mug in the center holder, she snatched up the diary and her purse and pushed open her door.

"You have got to be kidding me!" The bellowing call sounded from behind the wall of plexiglass that separated the squad room from the waiting area out front. It ushered from a towering man, broad-shouldered with brown, slicked-back hair and a scruffy beard that looked like it hadn't been trimmed in months. He charged doggedly through the room directly toward the locked door in front of Dani. A buzzer sounded as he reached it and he swept through, swiftly crossing the six-foot distance to her and wrapping her up in a bearhug so that her face was buried solidly in the chest of his blue uniform. He smelled of cheap cologne and sweet, pungent pipe tobacco.

"What in the world are you doing here?" Police Chief Bobby Killen asked, pulling back and revealing a beaming face as Dani sucked in a breath. "Big ol' fancy Boston cop showing her face in my station."

"Big ol' fancy Boston *detective* you mean," she replied, grinning.

"No! Seriously? Aw, Dani, that's great." The Chief signaled to the officer behind the front desk, who buzzed them back through to the squad room. He strode ahead of her, as if heralding the arrival of the star of a parade. "You hear that, guys?" he announced to the room in general. "It's *Detective* Danielle Lake now."

"We heard ya, Chief," said the officer who had buzzed them in. He tilted his head toward Dani in acknowledgment. "Congrats, Dani."

"Thanks, Mickey," she said, smiling broadly.

The Chief kept going, headed, she knew, straight for his office at the back. Of the half dozen desks in the squad room, only a couple were occupied at the moment, and Dani didn't know either of the officers. One, a female working on her computer, merely glanced up and nodded at Dani before returning to her screen. But the second, a man in plainclothes, locked eyes with her, cocking his head slightly as a small curve raised the corner of his mouth. He was raven-haired and clean-shaven, with a strong build that filled out his white button-down exactly as it had been meant to be. His eyes, as dark as his hair, continued tracking her as she followed the Chief.

Dani received this kind of attention sometimes—not in her own station so much, but sometimes when visiting others. She didn't like it, but it was what it was. Hoping to end the exchange, she offered him a little nod, which seemed to work.

He nodded in return, his gaze drifting back to the paperwork he was holding, although, as she passed him, out of the corner of her eye she thought she saw that the little curve at the corner of his mouth had stretched into a full smile.

*Men.*

~

"Good grief, Dani. You should know better." Chief Killen sat behind his desk, staring at the diary that now lay at the center of his blotter, secured in an evidence bag. He rubbed his hand across his beard before slapping it hard on the desk's surface. "You should have called as soon as you found it."

"I know, Chief." Dani felt even worse now than she had when sitting in the car. He was taking the news exactly as she feared he would. "But you've got to understand. I was in some kind of shock or something. I wasn't thinking straight. I mean, of all things...to find *her* diary? When I saw there was something down there, I thought maybe, drugs or something. You know, teens using the shed. And then, when the diary rolled out, I didn't know it was hers. I was just thinking some kid was using the place as a hideout and had stashed it down there—"

"Some kid, like Jennifer Cartwright?" he asked, his face screwing up and his eyebrows rising.

"No, not Jennifer. Like, some kid recently. Not a kid from thirteen years ago. Jennifer didn't even cross my mind."

"You should have called—"

"Would someone have come if I had? I mean, right then? It's a thirteen-year-old case which, according to everybody, has been long solved. Can you honestly say that dealing with it wouldn't have been pushed till morning? That you wouldn't have told me to just take it with me for safekeeping and come down here today?"

He eyed her from under narrowed lids. She knew that

scenario was a real possibility. Skye's population hovered around six thousand. At most, the Chief probably had three patrols running in the middle of the night and she was doubtful any of them would have been spared to deal with her non-emergency situation regarding an old case. Especially given that now, sitting here, watching his reaction, she was sure he would have wanted to handle it himself—and there wasn't much chance he would have traded the comfort of his easy chair and wife, Nancy, at well past eight for a dead girl's diary.

"Maybe," he finally said.

"Okay, then."

"But still—"

"But still, I should have called."

"And you've contaminated it. Your fingerprints will be all over it."

"When I opened it in the shed, I didn't know what it was. As soon as I did, the diary went back in the bag, which went in that bag," she said, pointing to her clear zip-top bag. "After that, I wore gloves when I touched any of it." She held up her hands in surrender. "I swear."

"What were you doing there anyway? I thought you hated that place. You told me you'd never been back there."

Dani shrugged. "All I can say is that I felt like it was time. With Mom and Dad gone, I've got enough burdens to carry. Enough ghosts. Maybe I just felt it was time to let that one go."

Chief Killen sniffed and shifted in his seat which groaned under the weight of his ample frame. "So did you read it?"

"Some." She explained how her initial review of the latter entries revealed a boyfriend Jennifer had been fighting with, but otherwise produced nothing notable, and that after starting back at the beginning, she found the entries to be lengthy and generally mundane. "It's a teenager, writing about teenage things. If there's a nugget hidden in there, it may take scouring the book several times to catch it."

"And you didn't read it all?" There was a note of surprise, and—unless she was just imagining it—disappointment in his voice.

"I planned to." Her face grew warm and she wondered if a sheepish expression had emerged there to match the embarrassment she felt. *Great detective I am, falling asleep on the evidence.* "Guess I was more exhausted than I realized," she offered weakly.

She studied him for a moment, trying to read the emotions behind his narrowed gaze. He leaned back, his chair creaking as it tilted toward the bookcase behind him. The oak shelves displayed a wide array of football paraphernalia—signed balls, banners and action shots—photos of Nancy and their six grandchildren, and the horses on his farm. He seemed to contemplate things for a moment, lacing and unlacing his fingers, then rocked forward, leaning his elbows on the desk.

"Don't beat yourself up. You had a full day of travel and the emotional gut punch of going to your parents' house—God rest 'em—and then finding this," he tapped the diary, "in *that* place. It's no wonder you passed out."

"Thanks," she said, and she meant it. His words eased at least some of the inadequacy she had been feeling. But now, she had to press him. "Chief, are you going to give it to him?"

"Who?"

"You know who."

His shoulders sagged. "I thought you were done with this."

"He didn't do it, Chief."

"Dani, you spent your last summers in high school interning here, chewing my ear off about how Dr. Beecher wasn't guilty and that we needed to get off our butts and prove it."

"He *isn't* guilty."

"A jury said he was. Jennifer's bracelet was found in his nightstand. They had a fight earlier on the day she died. His own daughter said she'd seen him go down to the riverbank, following after Jennifer and that he'd come back upset—"

"And his skin was found under her nails," Dani rattled off sharply.

"Exactly."

"I know the list. I've heard it a million times. But there are explanations for that evidence."

"Explanations which Beecher's attorney gave, but the jury didn't buy."

"He didn't have a motive," she said, her words clipped.

"He was obsessed with her and she wasn't having it."

"That was just speculation."

"Not after a jury believes it, it's not."

For thirteen years Dani had been confronted with these reasons, this "evidence" that proved Dr. Beecher—her friend, her mentor—had killed Jennifer Cartwright. For thirteen years, these reasons had made her blood boil because every single one of them was either circumstantial or could be explained another way—had, in fact, been explained by Dr. Beecher himself. But he was the target they had all settled on and no one would listen.

Today was no exception. Dani clenched the arm of her chair as she eyed the Chief. "You know you have to give it to his attorney."

Chief Killen sighed. "That's a decision for the D.A.'s office. They'll take a look and decide whether we have to hand it over to them." Though the original case had been initially investigated by the Skye P.D., it had been turned over to the county district attorney's office for prosecution.

Dani knew this answer was the best she was going to get from him at this point, so she left it. "What about the shed? I can take someone over there now, show you where I found it—"

"Not that we'll find anything after you traipsed all through there."

She tilted her head and felt her face sour. "That's not fair."

He ran a hand over his hair. "No. No, you're right, it's not. I get why you did what you did, I just...hope it didn't taint anything. I'll send Newton over to the Beecher property with you. He can secure it and see if it's worth calling forensics in."

A prickly heat crept up her neck. "*Worth* calling in? Seriously?"

"Dani, it's a closed case. Thirteen years closed. All his appeals have been exhausted—"

"Not when there's new evidence—"

"*If* there's new evidence."

"If?"

"Dani, no one wants this case reopened. This wound has finally healed for everyone. As best as it can, anyway. We've got to handle this carefully—quietly—so that no one gets hurt, or hopeful, unnecessarily. So, for now, just keep this to yourself, all right? It stays between you, me and Newton, okay?"

It was a true request, not a demand, because she wasn't a member of his department. He couldn't give her orders. She was a civilian who had found something and was free to talk about it if she chose—to the newspapers and to other potential interested parties. But she expelled a vexed breath and nodded.

"Thanks," he said.

"But," she added quickly, "I'm gonna need a favor from you."

He leaned back again, crossing his arms over his bulging middle, as his eyebrows rose dubiously toward the ceiling.

"Detective Danielle Lake, Boston P.D., meet Detective Chris Newton, Skye P.D.," Chief Killen said, standing with Dani behind the desk of the dark-haired officer who had watched her so intently when she had arrived. Detective Newton looked up and grinned profusely, revealing a captivating smile of gleaming teeth, and Dani felt a little bubble rise in her chest. Pushing back his chair with a screech, Detective Newton rose to a height of somewhere north of six feet, and extended a strong, tanned hand. Dani shook it, finding his grip firm, but gentle, not like some guys on the job who felt the need to prove something by squeezing the fire out of your hand on that first shake.

"It's Chris," he said.

"Dani," she replied, and unable to help herself, squeezed his hand a bit harder for good measure. "Nice to meet you." As before, his gaze locked onto hers, but not so that it was off-putting. Rather, it conveyed an assurance that at that moment she had his complete and sincere attention. There was some-thing almost mesmerizing about it, his eyes so dark brown they were nearly black, drawing her in like ebony pools, inviting her to dive in—

"I know you," he said.

She dropped his hand and stepped back, her head inclining to one side. "I don't think so."

"Yeah, I saw you. Yesterday. At Green's? You were at the end of the counter."

A rush of recognition flooded her.

*He's the guy in the T-shirt who came in. How did I not recognize him?* She mentally kicked herself over the lapse. Granted, he had cleaned up, shaven, and was dressed professionally and not in workout clothes, but still, all of the excitement over the diary had really put her off her game.

"Oh, right," Dani said, then felt her face flush as she real-ized she had just admitted she had not only noticed him, but *remembered* him. The corners of Detective Newton's mouth turned up again, this time stretching nearly to his eyes, confirming he had, in fact, picked up on that embarrassing little revelation. Her stomach turning, she scrambled to recover. "Hazard of the job, you know? Always watching the door."

"Uh-huh," he said, his lips now clamping together as if suppressing an even wider grin.

*Well, it's the truth.*

The Chief, seemingly oblivious to the awkward interaction going down right in front of him, proceeded to run through the details of the situation for Detective Newton. "So, I want you to head over there with Dani now and check it out. I don't want to draw attention and I don't want to mess this up, although I doubt it'll turn into much of anything other than a bit more heartache for Jennifer's parents. I'll get a warrant—shouldn't take long—so just go secure the scene until I call with the go-ahead."

"Got it, Chief," Detective Newton answered. He gathered a few things, tossed them in a duffel and slung it over his shoulder. "Beecher's house is still empty, right? No one to notify?"

Chief Killen nodded. "As far as I know, he's still holding it in trust for his kids."

"Actually, that shed belongs, or at least it used to belong, to the caretakers who lived in that house on the back of his property," Dani said.

"No one's there now. Those folks have been gone for ages. Died years ago."

"It's just sitting empty too?" Dani asked.

Chief Killen shrugged. "Beecher sold it to them when he went to prison. The husband died a few years after the murder —boating accident—and the wife died several after that, I think. If the shed's part of that lot, we'll need to get in touch with whoever owns it now. And I'll need to adjust the warrant. And, um," he crooked a finger at Detective Newton, "can I have a quick word?"

Leaving Dani at the detective's desk, the Chief and Detective Newton stepped back into the Chief's office. They were gone only a few minutes before the detective popped back out with the Chief in tow.

"All right," Detective Newton said, a cheerful light in his eyes. "You ready, Boston?" He extended a hand toward the front of the room, indicating that she should lead the way.

She snorted good-naturedly. "It's *Dani*, and yeah. Let's go." She had only advanced a few steps when Chief Killen called after her.

"And about that favor, Dani? That's between you and me, okay?"

Turning back toward him, she gave a two-fingered salute, then walked out, Detective Newton on her heels.

## 5

"So, you go way back with the Chief?" Detective Newton asked as he drove down Main Street, headed for the turnoff onto Dr. Beecher's gravel drive.

"All the way back," Dani answered from the passenger seat. "He and my parents have been—were—friends since high school."

"Huh. Must be nice to have those kinds of connections here."

"You don't, Detective?" she asked, glancing over. His black hair was cut short, but with just enough length so that his natural curl slightly flipped the tips up at the base of his neck. The olive cast of his tanned skin had a sort of Mediterranean quality about it, the kind of tone that never burned, just tanned perfectly the first time one stepped into the sun after winter. Not like Dani, who had to slather on SPF 50 for the first two months of summer, or risk a third-degree burn.

He shook his head and she caught the scent of something peaty, almost like whiskey, and some kind of spice. "Really, call me 'Chris,' and no, I'm not from here," he said. "I'm originally from St. Louis."

"I don't remember seeing you here before—at the station, I mean. I visit the Chief sometimes when I come home."

"Oh. Well, I've been here for about six years now. But, before making detective I would have been on patrol most of the time, so it's likely I was never around when you stopped by. Unfortunately."

He put a distinct emphasis on the word "unfortunately," but she ignored it. "So, how'd you get from St. Louis to our little town in the middle of nowhere?"

He chuckled. "A little town in the middle of nowhere was exactly what I was looking for. You're in Boston. You know how much crime goes down in a big city like that. I burned out on it in less than a year. I was searching for something smaller and came across a listing for a position in the Skye P.D. The rest is history."

Though he wasn't looking at her—his eyes were firmly fixed on the road ahead—she could tell from his profile that his grin was threatening to emerge again. She also couldn't help but notice that the sleeves of his white oxford shirt were rolled up to his biceps, which frankly looked like they were a little choked by the makeshift cuff. The ridiculous thought, *I wonder how much he can bench-press,* flitted through her brain, when she suddenly realized he was watching her, and snapped her gaze forward as a tingling sensation swept up her neck.

He chuckled softly. "It's all right, Boston."

"No, I was just wondering if I could out-bench you."

"Uh-huh."

"I was. And it's 'Dani,' I told you," she said, forcing an edge into her voice.

"Nope, sorry. It's 'Boston' now. Get used to it."

"Fine, then, *St. Louis.*"

"Nah. You're not going to be able to keep that up. And it just sounds silly when you do it."

She was trying to decide how it was possible for someone to

be equally irritating and charming at the same time when they came to the gravel drive leading to Dr. Beecher's estate. As he turned onto it, the sound of the grey rocks crunching beneath the tires filled the cabin, and Dani's thoughts shifted instantly, a vague, hollow sensation blanketing her.

"You okay?" he asked. The change in her must have been palpable.

"Yeah, fine. It's just...not my favorite place." The empty, three-story antebellum home of Dr. Thomas Beecher was visible through the oak-dotted grounds to their right, scrolling by slowly as they continued down the drive.

"I get it," he said. "The Chief gave me a little background info."

Dani straightened in her seat, her spine lengthening and her chin rising slightly. "Well, it doesn't matter. We've got a job to do, right?"

"That we do," he agreed.

By the time they had parked near the shed, Chief Killen had radioed that he had secured the warrant and green-lit the search. Chris pulled latex gloves and plastic shoe covers from his duffel, which they both adorned before heading inside the structure. Now Dani stood off to the side to avoid disturbing anything as she took him through last night's discovery.

"...and I just happened to see it when the light from my phone went through the gap in the floorboards." She pointed to the opening in the floor where the removed board had been. It still lay on the other side of the shed, exactly where it had landed the night before. "I pried it up and the thing practically flew out of my hands. It wasn't actually nailed down."

He looked at the board, then back at her. "Then what?"

"Once I realized what that diary was, the only thing I was thinking was that I needed to get out of here and get home." She held up a hand to shush him as he started to speak. "I know it goes against standard procedure. I know it wasn't the smartest thing to do. But I wasn't thinking like a cop at the time."

"You were thinking like the grown-up version of a fifteen-year-old girl who may have just found something to explain why her friend was murdered."

A rush of gratitude flooded her. She hadn't been expecting that kind of understanding from a stranger. "Exactly," she said.

"Look, I get it," he said, pushing himself up from his squatted position on the floor. "I wasn't here back then, but Jennifer Cartwright's murder is a well-repeated story in town, and so is your part in it. That had to have been horrible, and I'll bet finding that diary just brought it all back."

"It did." She had crossed her arms, and was idly rubbing her palms against her skin.

"It would have thrown me too Boston. At least you had the presence of mind to stick the diary back in the plastic. I'm not sure I would have." He brushed off his khakis and straightened the shoulder holster that held his service weapon. He sniffed and eyed her intently. "One thing I don't get is, what were you doing here? I mean, if this place bothers you so much—and believe me, I completely understand why it would—what were you doing out here after dark, or at all for that matter?"

"I've asked myself that a thousand times since last night. I've never set foot on this property since the day I found Jennifer's body. Not once. But with my parents passing recently and the house being empty—I don't know. That place didn't feel right either. I just started walking and ended up here."

His expression clouded. "By the way, I'm sorry—about your parents. I should have said earlier. The Chief mentioned it to me before we left. He said it was a car accident?"

She inhaled a heavy breath. "Drunk driver. He survived, they didn't."

After a quiet moment, he continued, the tone of his voice artificially upbeat, as if making a concerted effort to move past the subject. "Well, look, there's nothing else under the floor. At least not in that spot. We'll check the rest of the space beneath, of course. I'll get our crime scene investigator out here—I mean, it won't be fancy computer techs with all your upstart *CSI:Boston* doodads, but we'll get the job done. If there's something to find, we'll find it. But I wouldn't hold out much hope. You know as well as I do, if that diary was put there by Jennifer or someone else back in 1995, it's unlikely any trace evidence of them will still be here."

"But you'll let me know what you find?"

He cocked his head and let a wry smile slip. "Now, Boston, you know how that works. You'll have to talk to the Chief about that."

"Right. Talk to the Chief." She tried to fix her face to look sufficiently chastised about the overreach, but one way or another, she was getting that information, no matter what the Chief or Detective Chris Newton said.

# 6

"You went to that shed *alone* with Chris Newton?" Sasha's eyes were wide as she looked at Dani after picking up her two-year-old daughter's fork off the floor for the third time and putting it back on her high chair tray.

Sasha and her husband, Willett, Dani, Peter and Peter's wife, Amy, all sat around Sasha's farmhouse dining room table, halfway through a dinner that was getting colder by the minute.

"What do you mean, 'alone'?" Dani asked, her tone growing increasingly weary. It had been such a long day, and though she had not noticed until now, sitting still in this chair for the last thirty minutes had made it quite clear just how tired she was.

She hadn't left the shed until around two thirty, when Chris was finally securing it with "DO NOT CROSS" tape, after watching Skye P.D.'s one-person CSI team take care of business. After that she had let Chris take her back to the station to get her car, then spent three draining hours just *beginning* the task of sorting through her parents' belongings. By six o'clock, she had barely made a dent, gave up and headed over to Sasha's, completely ravenous because with all the activity she had forgotten to eat lunch, a bad habit of hers.

But, as usual, Peter and Amy were late and they had to wait until nearly seven to start. At that point, all Dani wanted to do was eat, so she made a point of finishing most of her pasta before mentioning a word about anything that had happened the night before or since. Once she did, though, the meal had come to a full stop, and now, after a first pass through the events of the last twenty-four hours, they all hovered over half-finished plates of beef stroganoff, gob-smacked.

"I can't believe it," Peter said.

"And on top of all that," Sasha drawled, a knowing grin materializing on her face, "Chris Newton."

Dani snorted. "That's what you want to talk about? Not what I found in Jennifer's diary?"

"You told us everything, right?" Sasha replied in her defense. "You said there wasn't anything in the diary."

"No," Willett corrected, tossing his wife a wry smile, "she said she didn't find anything in it before she turned it over to the police."

"So, hold up," Peter interrupted, spreading his hands wide. "I still can't get over that we were sitting here, eating stroganoff and salad and talking about Sasha's reunion progress for thirty minutes, like everything's normal, and *then* you drop this bomb. This is huge, Dani!"

"I know, but...I was starving," Dani explained sheepishly. "If I'd started when we sat down, I wouldn't have been able to eat."

"I just can't believe you didn't rush right in here and start spilling it. Or, call us earlier, for that matter. I mean, you've been obsessed with this for *thirteen years*—"

For just a second, Dani thought she caught the tiniest flash of something behind Peter's eyes.

"Maybe," Amy started, laying a hand on Peter's arm, "Dani just needed a little time to process it." A licensed counselor, Amy worked with Peter at the Skye Youth Center, and right now she seemed to be using her skills to temper her husband.

Sasha's two-year-old, Alana, picked that moment to fling an egg noodle across the table with her spoon, where it landed with a plop in Dani's water glass.

"I'm not mad," Peter said, apparently reading and interpreting his wife's reaction. "I'm worried. It's just not normal for someone who's been this wrapped up in something for this long to keep quiet about it for even a minute. I just worry that maybe she's not handling it as well as she's wanting us to believe."

"I'm fine. *I promise,*" Dani said when Peter continued peering at her skeptically. "And besides, there isn't anything else for me to do. Chris has charge of the investigation and Chief Killen has people looking at the diary. And, anyway, I doubt it'll come to anything. Not after all this time."

"So, *Chris* took over the investigation...not *Officer Newton,*" Sasha teased.

"He *is* one of Skye's most eligible bachelors, Dani," Amy piped in, tossing Dani a conciliatory smile.

Willett's face screwed up as he shook his head. "Do not encourage her, Amy."

"What?" Sasha asked innocently, fooling no one. "She's single, he's single. She's pretty and he's—"

"Gorgeous," Amy said, and all three women snorted while the men rolled their eyes.

Dani shook her finger at Sasha. "No match-making, Sash. I mean it. You know why I'm here."

Sasha's shoulders dropped. "I know. But would it be the worst thing in the world if you had to spend a *little* time with a handsome, strong, brave—"

"Enough already, Sasha. You're gonna give a man a complex," Willett said, tossing his napkin on his plate.

"Aww," Sasha replied, leaning over to kiss Willett's cheek. "He's got nothing on you, baby."

Dani's heart warmed. It was nice to see her friends so happy and content in their marriages. She would have given anything for it to have been like that for her. Anything to still be with Finn, for him to be at this table with her now, laughing and carrying on and kissing her on the cheek. A baby in a high chair beside them...

*Stop. He left you. Take off the rose-colored glasses. Focus on the here and now.*

And here and now she had friends who loved her, who worried about her, who wanted her to be whole and happy—

"Maybe you could bring him to the reunion," Sasha spouted.

"What?" Dani asked incredulously, nearly drowned out by the shouts of Sasha's four-year-old son, Trent, who came running in, circling the table and making engine noises, his arms outstretched like an airplane.

"You. Chris Newton. Come on, it could be fun—"

Dani leveled a cold, steel stare at her best friend in the world. "Not another word, Sasha Mason. You hear me? Not. Another. Word."

AFTER READING TRENT A STORY, Dani had finally dragged herself out of Sasha's, landing at home with barely enough energy to drop into her father's leather recliner in the living room. Tilting her head back, she yanked on the spring bar that deployed the footrest, rocketing her feet upward. She inhaled, exhaled, and surveyed the long, narrow room, typical of most ranch-style homes. Faux red brick covered the wall behind the entertainment center, and in the corner to its right was the free-standing wood fireplace with its exposed, black-painted flume rising through the ceiling. A panoramic window took up most of the exterior wall, and opposite that was an L-shaped, grey microfiber couch. The cardboard boxes Dani had purchased at Lowe's were assembled and stacked in the center of the room, except for three open ones on the floor which were filled to varying degrees with her mother's and father's belongings.

*An entire afternoon, and all I managed was three lousy boxes.*

The whole point of her presence here, other than the slight diversion of the reunion, was to complete the clearing of the house. All the jewelry and easily portable valuables had been removed at the time of the funeral when she and Nikki had gone through the house, trying to make a plan. Anything Nikki had wanted, but couldn't take back with her on the plane, she had marked with a sticky note. She had said she would come back and help box it all up for shipment, but of course, that hadn't happened. Now it was all up to Dani.

She had decided that the most effective way to tackle this thing was to take it one room at a time. So the living room was where she had begun that afternoon—pulling vases and frames and anything else Nikki had tagged. But even after packing up Nikki's bits, there was so much left. Afghans, throw pillows and books, ceramic figurines, an ancient VCR...

*Thank God for Estate Settlers.* For a fee, the company out of Birmingham would come to her parents' home and handle the distribution of the personal property. Dani's job was to divide it all into "Donate," "Sell," "Toss," and "Keep" boxes. Then Estate Settlers would dispose of it accordingly. Her stomach soured at the thought of someone else, some other family, living here—painting over her mother's favorite buttercup-colored paint, tearing out the emerald green carpet in the living room, ripping out her father's built-in pine shelves...

Hot tears formed as Dani's eyes traced the shelves it had taken her father two months to build, stain and install. Her gaze fell across the top shelf, home to the eagle figurines her father had collected—"Eagle Perched," "Eagle Flying," "Eagle Clenching Trout," and so on. For as long as she had lived there, those figurines had been displayed in a perfectly straight line, evenly spaced, in order of acquisition. They had been her father's prized possessions, and were one of the few things Dani was definitely taking back to Boston—

She shot up out of the chair and marched over to the shelves until she was standing directly in front of the figurines. "Eagle Flying" was crooked, its base turned just slightly out of line with the others. Earlier today, feeling a bit punchy after several hours at it, she had put her own sticky notes on Dad's eagles as a sarcastic nod to Nikki. But she hadn't moved the figurines. And they were heavy, solid, ceramic-cast things. Simply tapping a sticky note onto one wouldn't have moved it.

*Would it?*

Tendrils of frustration tightened in her chest as she dug at the muddled corners of her brain, trying to remember if she had moved the eagle, picked it up to look at it, or something.

*No.* Almost certainly not.

She turned around, now surveying her surroundings, not sentimentally, but analytically.

*Had someone been in the house after I left for dinner at Sasha's?*

Her mind firing, she walked slowly to the kitchen, scanning for...well, anything out of place. Part of her felt ridiculous, like she was overreacting after the events in the shed, knowing her senses were probably on high alert, her nerves still raw—then she saw her coffee mug in the sink. The mug she had left on the counter.

*Hadn't I?*

Her gaze flicked to the kitchen table. The estate papers she had left there were perfectly stacked and straightened. Almost too perfectly. She had perused them earlier in the day, and while she hadn't scattered them, she didn't remember tapping the edges into square alignment either.

A switch in her brain flipped and she ran to her bedroom, grabbed her service pistol from beneath her pillow and began sweeping through the house room by room. But after several minutes of inspecting every closet, under every bed, and behind every curtain, the house proved empty.

Her heart thudding, she returned to her bedroom, this time not looking for an intruder, but for anything that seemed out of place. It jumped out at her almost immediately.

*My suitcase.*

Dani tended to live out of her suitcase when traveling—clothes tossed in and out and around it rather than in drawers—so it wasn't unusual for there to be an unorganized pile of stuff cast ring-like around it. But something about the unpacked, haphazard pile of clothing looked somehow different. Instead of being on top, the shirt she had worn yesterday was peeking out from beneath a pair of pants she hadn't worn yet. But had she left it like that?

Maybe.

*Maybe not.*

The thought of someone rifling through something so intimate as her clothing left her feeling distinctly violated. Disquiet surging within her, she started back toward her parents' bedroom to check more closely for anything amiss, when the doorbell rang. The trilling sound sent a jolt of electricity through her and her heart leapt into her throat. Clutching her chest with one hand while still holding her pistol in the other, she worked to catch her breath as she made her way to the front door.

She pressed her eye against the peephole and saw Detective Chris Newton standing on the other side. Her breathing slowed considerably, the tension that had gripped her easing as she opened the door.

"Hi?" she said, the word more of a question than a greeting, sure that the puzzlement she felt must be visible on her face.

"Hey, Boston," he said, rocking back and forth on his Dockers, his hands jammed into his front pockets. He had changed from his work clothes—showered even, by the look of his damp hair—into a short-sleeved forest-green polo and jeans.

"What...are you doing here?" She noticed the clipped tone of her voice, and he must have too, because a mild frown replaced the soft smile he had started with.

"Uh, well, I guess...I wanted to make sure you were okay. I know today was rough on you."

"You could have called." She knew she sounded rude. She didn't mean to. But she was spooked and the last thing she had expected was a visitor.

His eyes narrowed as he clearly seemed to pick up on her frosty vibe. "Yeah," he drawled, "but...I didn't." He leaned back, as if attempting to get a better look at her. "Are you sure you're okay?"

Ignoring his question, she focused on the area behind him. The yard and street were empty, the solitary streetlamp at the bottom of her drive revealing no one lurking around who might have been responsible for the suspected tampering inside. It wasn't surprising. She had been at Sasha's for hours. If someone had been in the house, they were probably long gone.

"Boston?" His tone was darker, ripe with real concern. "What's wrong?"

"Uh, nothing. Sorry," she said, then sighed. "You want to come in?"

His brow furrowed. "Yeah. Okay."

She urgently motioned him inside. When she turned after shutting and locking the door behind him, his gaze flashed to her right hand.

"Why are you walking around with your service weapon?"

She looked down at the pistol in her hand. "Oh. I was just... well, I thought that maybe someone had been here earlier. While I was gone. I was just doing a sweep."

His eyes widened and he took a step back, something about his posture becoming demonstrably more formal. "As in, you think someone broke in?"

She nodded and his hand moved to hover over the holster of his own service weapon, his thumb flipping open the restraining strap. "Have you cleared it?"

"Yeah, I cleared it. I just finished when you rang."

"You want me to go through it—"

"No. Look, I'm sorry I was short with you, I just, I was coming off searching the house and the bell startled me." She purposefully fixed a smile on her face. "It was nice of you to come check on me. You want some coffee or something? Decaf?"

"If you're sure. Sounds good."

He followed her to the kitchen, dropping into one of the chairs at the table while she set her weapon down on the counter, then moved around the kitchen, preparing the pot of coffee.

"You really didn't have to come over," she repeated. "You could've called."

"Yeah, but...the Chief happened to mention your address and it seemed like a waste of information not to use it."

"Mmm-hmm," she answered, turning away so that he couldn't see the slip of a grin on her face.

"So what made you think that someone's been here?" he said.

"Little things. Stuff that may have been moved." She pointed to the cup in the sink, then the papers on the table. "I think I left the cup out and that stack messier. And I'm pretty sure my suitcase has been gone through, though I couldn't swear to it."

"Nothing taken?"

She shook her head. "I don't think so. It wasn't destructive. It feels more like..." She trailed off, and felt her face flush.

"What?"

"It sounds crazy, but it just feels like someone—if there even was a someone—just wanted to check me out. Does that sound nuts?" she asked, setting a steaming mug in front of him and pushing the sugar bowl in his direction as she sat down.

He dumped two spoonfuls in. "It doesn't sound crazy. That sounds like a stalker."

"Why would I have a stalker in Skye?" she asked, blowing across the surface of her own mug. Steamy spirals rose from the cup, accompanied by a rich aroma that aided in settling her nerves.

"What about a trespasser? Somebody that's been coming in here while the house has been empty? How long's that been?"

She pursed her lips, considering that possibility. "Since March. But I've had an agent checking on it every couple of weeks, walking through, making sure there aren't any problems —she would have noticed if someone had been here."

Dani took a sip and swallowed, the heat sliding into her stomach. Sitting here now, talking about it with another person, she was starting to feel a little ridiculous and shades of doubt began to set in. Had things in the house been different? Truly? Or was she just exhausted and forgetful, discombobulated with everything that was going on. It would be understandable.

"Maybe I'm wrong. Maybe it's all in my head. I *am* really tired. I've had a couple of really long, weird days."

"You're a trained detective, Boston. If you think someone was here, someone probably was."

She appreciated the vote of confidence, but it didn't make her feel better. "Well, at this point, I think I'd prefer it if maybe I was a little off-kilter and there was actually nothing to worry about."

"I'm just saying, trust your instincts." He brought his mug to his lips, which were thin but strong, accenting a sharp, square jaw. He drank, looking over the rim, never taking his eyes from her.

She held his gaze. "You didn't really just come to check on me, did you? I mean, if you did, it's fine, but it seems like a lot of effort for someone you just met."

Now his eyes left hers, drifting down to the cup where he tapped a finger against the handle. "No, I didn't just come for that. I mean, I did want to see if you were okay, but...I also thought you'd want to know what we found."

Dani sat up, her wavering focus suddenly laser sharp. "What did you find?"

Almost instantly his lips parted, stretching wide to reveal an awkward, remorseful grin. "Oh, I, uh, probably should have phrased that better. What we found was really, well—nothing. Trish—the crime scene investigator—said that there weren't any useful footprints—other than yours from the other night, and no fingerprints that she could find—"

"Except for mine from the other night," Dani chimed in.

Chris nodded. "Except for those. No hair, no blood, no fluids, nothing. The animals have clearly been in and out of there for ages and there wasn't anything else in the space under the floor where you found the diary."

"So, a big, fat zero."

"Well, it has been thirteen years. We don't have the labs back on the plastic bag or the diary yet, but I wouldn't hold out too much hope after so much time and exposure."

"What about the diary itself—the entries I mean?"

"They've got someone in the D.A.'s office going through it."

"Well, I can't imagine it would take them beyond tomorrow to finish it."

"Depends what they have going on. You've got to remember that this case is closed. They're short-handed and loaded up with cases that are very much *not* closed yet."

"I can't believe they wouldn't want to dive into a decade-plus-old murder."

"As far as they're concerned, this decade-plus-old murder's been solved for just as long. They got their man. This diary just complicates things. You may be glad that you found it, but I don't think you'll find a lot of others who are. I don't think they're in any rush to turn over stones." He drained the last of his cup and plopped it on the table with a thud. "So, I've checked on you, I've brought you up to speed and I've finished my coffee. I think I've exhausted my excuses to be here, so," his chair squeaked against the tile as he pushed it back, "I am gonna go. Leave you to get some rest." He pointed at the cup, then the dishwasher. "Should I—"

"No, just leave it."

She rose and followed him to the front door. Just as he put a hand on the knob, he turned back to her. "Listen," he said, exhaling, "I know you can take care of yourself and all—"

"Preach."

He chuckled. "But I can arrange for a patrol car to cruise by here a couple of times a day. And at night. Just to be sure."

She waved him off. "Nah. Honestly, after talking with you I think I'm just being paranoid. I think if I can get a good night's sleep and a break from obsessing about this case, I'll be fine."

"So, no Jennifer Cartwright tomorrow?"

"Tomorrow's a packing day, and I'm helping a friend decorate for our class reunion on Saturday."

"Sasha, right? I know Willett from the Grille. I eat lunch there all the time. He mentioned she's in charge of the whole thing."

Willett was the proprietor of The Skye Grille, one of the most popular eateries in town. It wasn't surprising that Chris would frequent it, but it did surprise Dani that Willett hadn't mentioned anything about that when they were talking about

Chris at dinner. "Oh, right. She mentioned she knew you," Dani said.

His face beamed mischievously. "You and Sasha were talking about me?"

"We were talking about the diary and the shed. You just happened to be the person that went there with me."

"Ahh. And so you're part of the Class of '98, huh? That reunion's your shindig?"

"Yeah. It's why I'm handling this now," she waved a hand at the boxes, "instead of coming earlier. Two birds, and all that."

"The Chief said your parents were great people."

She smiled. "They were, thanks." She cocked her head. "You and the Chief were talking about me?"

"We were talking about the diary. You just happened to be the person who found it."

She laughed, closing her eyes and tilting her head as if to say, *touché.*

"You know, if you need help with those boxes or anything, moving or loading them—"

"I've hired a company for that," she replied.

"Oh. Well, even if you just need them shifted around, I'd be happy to help."

"Okay, thanks."

At that, he unceremoniously opened the front door and walked out, heading down the paved path to his Dodge Ram truck parked in the driveway. She continued holding the door open, leaning against its frame, the crickets chirping in a rising and falling chorus and the warm night breeze fluttering over her skin.

When he was about halfway down the path, she called out to him. "Officer Newton?"

He stopped, waited a few dramatic seconds with his back to her, then turned.

"Yeeeesss?"

"I thought you said I'd have to go through the Chief for information about your findings."

"I said that?" he asked with exaggerated innocence, his artificial, wide-eyed expression highlighted by the glare from the streetlamp.

She nodded vigorously.

"Hmm. Well, if I'd stuck to that, I would've had even less of a reason to come by, wouldn't I?"

She grinned. "I guess so."

He wrinkled his nose, squeezing his eyes shut and nodding in superior acknowledgment, then twisted away from her, continuing down the path. He threw a hand up over his shoulder. "See you later, Boston. Get some sleep," he called out, then climbed into his truck and drove away.

# 7

―――――――

ut sleep was not in Dani's immediate future. If she had
been thinking more clearly, on her way home she
would have picked up some Red Bull, but as it was, all
she had was her dad's coffee. So she poured out the pot of decaf
and brewed a whole pot of high-octane, double strength,
caffeinated-to-the-last-drop java that, with any luck, would
keep her up all night.

She considered which of her options was least likely to
break her back or allow her to drift off to sleep, finally settling
on sitting on the living room floor in front of the coffee table.
After moving her mother's silk daisy arrangement off of it, she
propped a few pillows between her and the couch for support,
parked herself on the floor and surveyed the tabletop. On the
left sat the stout mug of coffee on a coaster her parents had
picked up in Memphis that read, "Elvis Has Left The Building."
To the right was her service revolver. And directly in front of
her, printed in black ink on eight-and-a-half by eleven-inch
paper, was a photocopy of Jennifer Cartwright's diary.

Dani ran a hand over the thick stack, the paper slick against
it, not suffering even the slightest bit of guilt over making the

copy at the Office Hut before going to see Chief Killen that morning.

There was no way she could have turned the diary over without ensuring herself an opportunity to read through it completely. Since it was too long to get through before turning it in to the Chief—something that, from a procedural perspective, needed to happen as soon as possible—her only option had been to make a copy for herself.

There were other reasons too. Having a copy gave her some leverage, some power, just in case things stalled and she needed to be able to put some pressure on the authorities. Based on the Chief's and Chris's comments it sounded like no one was in any particular hurry to wade through it, or to address any potential questions it might raise.

*Well, I'm not having it.*

She was getting through this thing tonight. At least one full pass. And then she would know.

Dani had been dying to get to the diary all day, but when she hadn't returned to the house until nearly three, she realized that she had to get some packing done first if she wanted to stay on schedule and be ready when Estate Settlers came. She had known that if she opened the diary, she wouldn't have been able to put it down, so she forced herself to work until it was time to go to Sasha's. Chris's visit had delayed her a bit longer, but now there was nothing standing in her way.

She glanced at the other item lying on the coffee table: the file Chief Killen had given her which contained a copy of all the documents related to the initial investigation into Jennifer Cartwright's murder. It was a closed case, so it wasn't a violation of any rule to let her look it over, but it wasn't typically allowed. She had asked him for it as a favor, citing her need to gain closure. Which was the truth, but not exactly in the way he thought.

He had handed it to her, commenting that he hoped it

would help her finally put this obsession to rest. But her intention was to use it to break the case wide open, find a trail leading to the real murderer, and in *that* way, get closure. With any luck, comparing the evidence in the file to the entries in the diary would reveal something that pointed to someone other than Dr. Beecher as Jennifer's killer.

Determination fueling her, she tossed back a gulp of coffee, opened the diary to where she had left off the night before, and started reading.

~

*January 27, 1995*
*Dear Diary,*
*I got invited to Jason's party. I want to go, but Kendall doesn't because Andy will be there...*

*January 28, 1995*
*Dear Diary,*
*Well, of course, Kendall and Andy got back together at the party. I'm really worried about her. She tells me it's fine...*

*...*

*February 8, 1995*
*Dear Diary,*
*The Sadie Hawkins dance is coming up and I don't know who to ask. Sometimes I feel so...so...lonely. I guess everyone goes through that but it seems like no one really knows me or understands me. I'm thinking about asking Nathan. I don't know. But I know what I'm wearing. I got this amazing sweater at the Gap and I found a suede skirt that will go perfectly with my Liz Claiborne flats...*

...

*February 19, 1995*
*Dear Diary,*
*I got a C on my English test today. I don't know what*
*happened. I studied soooo hard. Mom and Dad won't be*
*happy. I'll ask Mr. Rheardon if I can do extra credit. I can't*
*have it dropping my average, not if I want a scholarship...*

...

*March 4, 1995*
*Dear Diary,*
*Our church youth group served at the veterans' home again*
*today. Mr. Crenshaw was so happy to see me. I brought him*
*chocolate chip cookies again—he says they're his favorite. I*
*love the way he smiles when I visit. And he tells the best*
*stories...*

...

*March 18, 1995*
*Dear Diary,*
*Sometimes I sit at the lunch table and look around at the girls*
*with me and wonder if any of them are really my friends.*
*Sometimes I hear them whispering, and sometimes I hear my*
*name. Kendall's the only one I really trust. I think most of*
*them just hang out with me because I'm a cheerleader or*
*whatever...*

Dani yawned and ran a hand over her hair, catching it in
her fingers and twirling it, stretching a piece across her mouth.
She glanced at the clock on the mantel. Twelve thirty. Three

hours and she had only gotten through March. The girl was prolific. At least one page each day, though usually more. And so far none of it had shed any light on what had happened to her.

What it had done, however, was introduce Dani to the girl that Jennifer Cartwright had been. Not the girl Dani knew from school—the popular, smart, got-it-all-together cheerleader that she had seen on the outside—but rather, the Jennifer on the inside, the insecure teenager who wanted to be understood, but never felt like she was. Who liked spending time with people and making them feel better, and who tried to look out for her friend's best interests. Who was worried about a C and what it might do to her grade point average. Who was lonely because she believed that most of her friends didn't really like her for who she was.

They had been more alike than Dani had realized at fifteen. Their problems might have varied in specifics or degree, but so much was the same—the insecurity, the fear of the future, the loneliness, the need to be a part of something real. It was hard for everyone, and it had been hard for Jennifer too.

Dani took another long sip of coffee, then went back to flipping pages. It was more of the same—angst and clothes and girl drama—until she reached the entry for April 21, 1995. Her breath caught in her chest as she read the same entry three times.

*April 21, 1995*
*Dear Diary,*
*I know a secret.*

*I know a secret.* The discovery energized Dani as she stared at the page, but Jennifer's lack of elaboration was maddening. The space beneath this single, potent sentence was completely blank. How was that possible? The girl could write a two-page dissertation on the merits of regular denim versus acid-washed, but on this pivotal issue, she had nothing else to say? Slightly annoyed, Dani kept reading, and to her relief was rewarded two entries later.

> *April 23, 1995*
> *Dear Diary,*
> *It's all I can think about. I couldn't hold it in anymore. I asked her—I just told her I had a feeling. I didn't tell her I'd seen them together—and she denied everything. But I don't believe her. I think he's a creep. An absolute creep. But I can't prove it, and what if I'm wrong? I don't think I am—I know what I saw—but I don't know what to do...*

Who was the "creep" and who was the "her" Jennifer had talked to who denied everything?

Dani grabbed her legal pad and jotted down the relevant dates along with notes about their content. Then she opened the case file, removed the summaries and reports and spread them out across the table. During an earlier inspection of the file, she noticed that the diary was mentioned in several of the reports as missing. She thought this would have made the investigators more anxious to quickly review the diary now that it had been found, not less so—unless, of course, they were afraid that the information it contained would undermine their original investigation and the jury's conviction, a concern both the Chief and Chris seemed to confirm by their comments.

Now she made a quick scan of the same investigation documents looking for, one, any mention of any "secret" Jennifer may have been keeping, and, two, any person—maybe the "creep"—that had worried her. But there was nothing of the sort recorded anywhere in the witness statements, reports or summaries.

From the looks of it, this was all new information. Hope

surged in the depths of Dani's spirit. Maybe there was a chance for Dr. Beecher after all.

# 8

April 24, 1995

*Dear Diary,*

*I think he knows. I think he saw me that day. I know she didn't, but I thought he might have seen me right before I ran out, and now I think I'm right. For a while now he's been trying too hard, smiling too much—it's so creepy. I won't smile back or anything, and I think he's finally changed tactics. Now he won't look at me anymore unless he has to. You know how you can tell when someone is avoiding you? Well, he is...*

*...*

*May 1, 1995*

*Dear Diary,*

*Dr. and Mrs. Beecher asked me to work as their nanny this summer. Their full-time nanny is leaving in May and with him being a doctor and her being a lawyer, there won't be anyone to watch the kids all summer. I am really excited. It's not that far from home so I can just ride my bike over. They* *said they'll pay me $150 a week! The kids are pretty easy too, Sam's four and Caitlin's six. I'll save soooo much money!...*

A pang of sadness struck Dani as she read these words. So that was how it had started. The Beechers asked Jennifer to be their nanny and she had ended up dead on their property just two months later. If only Jennifer had said no. If only they hadn't asked. Or would it have made a difference at all? Would she still have been murdered, but her body hidden somewhere else?

*May 4, 1995*
*Dear Diary,*
*I HAVE MET HIM...*

It was two in the morning when Dani read this entry that finally introduced the mysterious boyfriend. The boyfriend Jennifer wrote about in the July entries, whom she had been fighting with just days before she died. Dani sat up straight, blinked furiously to shake off the sleepiness pressing down on her, and plunged forward.

*...Well, not "met" him, really. But I've found him. I've known him for a long time—known who he is, I mean, but I've never really seen him, never really noticed him until now. And now, he's all I can think about. He is so smart. And funny. And he makes me feel safe. I can't wait to see him tomorrow. And the next day, and the next...*

*...*

*May 6, 1995*
*Dear Diary, Can you love someone after two days? Is that possible? He says he loves me. I think I love him too. But I*

*don't know if they will understand. I told him that we have to keep this a secret for now. He said he was okay with that. My parents wouldn't like this at all. They wouldn't like him. But I don't care. He's everything now. My guy. My whole world...*

...

*May 10, 1995*
*Dear Diary,*
*He is so amazing...*

...

*May 20, 1995*
*Dear Diary,*
*I want to be with him every second, but I can't even talk to him on the phone because my parents will see the number. He wants us to tell our parents. He's tired of having to keep it from everyone at school so I can avoid drama at home, but my parents won't get it. He says his parents will be fine with it and I said his parents aren't the problem. He says we can't keep going on like this because it isn't fair and it makes him feel terrible about himself. He says it makes him feel like I'm ashamed of him. I told him that's crazy and I didn't want to talk about it anymore...*

...

*May 22, 1995*
*Dear Diary, Today he gave me a ring. A silver band of twisted vines. He says it's to remind me of him when we are apart, or when we're in the same room, but have to pretend we aren't together. He still thinks we should tell our parents,*

*but I'm not ready. This ring is my favorite thing in the whole world. I'll never take it off...*

Every entry from there forward went on and on, page after page, about how wonderful "he" was and how they would be together forever. A boyfriend that Dani had never heard of— not at school, not before the murder and not after. Now that she had read those investigative reports through several times, she was absolutely sure that there was no mention in them whatsoever of a boyfriend, secret or otherwise.

A secret, a boyfriend and a "creep." Maybe the "secret" Jennifer had mentioned was a reference to the creep, but in any event, all of it was apparently unknown to the investigators. Scribbling furiously, Dani added more notes to her list, then kept reading. The entries continued to rave about the boyfriend —cute, sweet, gorgeous, his hair, his car, his favorite movies, the sweet things he said. Jennifer had catalogued all the places they met where no one would see them together. At school they would find ways to cross paths, sit in the library on opposite sides of the same table, etcetera. Then once summer came they would meet at the park by the ballfields, or at his house— because his parents both worked during the day—or at the shed by the river at Dr. Beecher's—

*The shed. They had met at the shed.*

So the boyfriend would have known about the thick mounds of honeysuckle growing along the fence just a few dozen yards from that shed. Thick, dense mounds that could hide anything. Even a body. Cold dread, sharp like shards of ice, pierced Dani's insides as she kept reading.

All the way through June, the entries about the boyfriend continued, all sugar and sunshine, along with the more mundane tidbits of Jennifer's life—a new pair of shoes, a trip to see a cousin in Georgia, regret over breaking some jewelry her grandmother had given her, a fight with her mother, and so on.

She even wrote about her job at Dr. Beecher's, and had nothing but good things to say. Both Dr. and Mrs. Beecher were kind. The kids were sweet, a little energetic, but sweet. It was easy money. It was a perfect teenage summer.

Then came June 26th.

*June 26, 1995*
*Dear Diary,*
*Today I saw the creep at the movies—fifteen miles away in Northport! Amber drove us—I can't wait to turn 16 too—He didn't see me, but I saw him. He was in a car, parked in the shadows down the side of the building. And I saw who he was with. It's clear what's going on—now I know I wasn't wrong before—and now he's trying it with someone else. I'm not going to tell her, though. I didn't tell Amber either. It won't help. It makes me sick just thinking about it. I don't know how he's kept this a secret from everyone. But someone needs to know. Someone needs to stop him. I told my guy about the creep, but he isn't sure what I should do either...*

*June 27, 1995*
*Dear Diary,*
*I did it. I confronted the creep. I went to his house and told him that I knew what was going on and that I was going to tell. He told me no one would believe me for obvious reasons. They would think I made it up. Maybe he's right. What if they don't believe me? Maybe I should just keep my mouth shut, otherwise I could really get hurt...*

*June 28, 1995*
*Dear Diary,*
*It's sooooo hot, I wish it would rain. All I can think about is what I should do. It's starting to scare me. I think he was following me today. I went in Goody's to find a swimsuit for*

*July 4th and saw him standing outside on the sidewalk when I looked up. He was just staring at me through the glass, until he finally just walked away. What if he starts stalking me?...*

*June 29, 1995*
*Dear Diary,*
*The creep called. He actually called my house when no one was home. How did he know I was alone? I want to do something, but I don't know what. As soon as I figure out who I can trust, I'm telling...*

*June 30, 1995*
*Dear Diary,*
*I can't think about this anymore. It's making me crazy. I don't know what to do. I have to stop thinking about it for a while. I just have to...*

*...*

*July 4, 1995*
*Dear Diary,*
*I spent the whole day at my cousin Ellie's lake house. It was a beautiful day. It was a good chance to get away and just forget...*

*...*

*July 6, 1995*
*Dear Diary,*
*We finally had it out—a horrible fight over how he thinks I'm making him feel like nothing. Like he doesn't matter, which is crazy! I told him he's being ridiculous, but he stormed off and he hasn't called me since. I waited for him at*

*the shed like we planned, but he didn't come. I really need to talk to him...*

*July 7, 1995*
*Dear Diary,*
*He finally called and we are still fighting. I told him that I want to talk it through but he says there isn't anything to talk about unless I'm ready to tell everyone. I don't care about other people knowing. I just know what my parents will do if they find out. They will not take it well. Especially not my dad. But he promised to meet me tomorrow at the shed. It'll be easy for me to slip away and no one will know. I have to make him understand and we really need to talk about everything, not just us. I really need to know what he thinks.*

*July 8, 1995*
*Dear Diary,*
*IT'S SO HOT. I can't stop sweating. I found those purple thistles near the road...*

*So this weekend, Kendall and I are definitely going to the movies...*

*He and I are supposed to meet after I get off work this after-noon. I've lied and told Mom I'm spending the night at Kendall's so I don't have to go home after work or be home by curfew in case this takes a long time. I might actually spend the night at Kendall's, but I'm not going to ask Kendall about it yet, because I don't know what's going to happen. I don't want her asking questions if something changes. Kendall's mom won't care if I just show up late. She's pretty cool that way. I'm so worried that he won't show up at all. What if he doesn't? What if he breaks up with me? I don't know what I'll do without him. He has to meet me...he just has to...*

The last entry was only half a page, likely written just hours before Jennifer breathed her last. The diary didn't name names. It didn't spell out precise motives. But it offered suspects and secrets and proof that there were others beside Dr. Beecher who had ties and issues with Jennifer, and maybe even reasons for wanting her dead.

In short, it changed everything.

# 9

"This changes nothing," Chief Killen said, dropping into his desk chair.

Sitting in the chair opposite him, Dani clenched her fists, trying to maintain her composure. It was barely eight thirty in the morning and she had rushed over to the station to share what she had found, expecting that he would be surprised, shocked, concerned—anything other than this. Anything other than indifferent.

"How can you say that? It changes everything!"

"Not according to the D.A.'s office."

Heat gathered at Dani's collar. She held up a hand and began counting on her fingers. "There's a secret boyfriend she was fighting with. An apparently damaging secret she was keeping about someone that she was considering exposing. *And,* that someone seems to have begun stalking her at the end. All this just days before she was murdered. How does that change nothing?"

Chief Killen leaned back, his chair giving a hearty squeak. "Because the D.A. says none of it's exculpatory. It's a closed case. And you know this isn't the first time we've had someone else to look at—there was that field hand, the migrant worker the caretakers hired that summer who took off right before she was found. But the evidence linked Jennifer to Dr. Beecher, not to the migrant worker and not to some boyfriend or stalker, either."

"But this gives them two other suspects that—according to the file you gave me—no one ever knew about. How can the D.A. be sure there isn't evidence out there linking *them* to the murder, if no one even knew to look into them before?"

Chief Killen's eyes narrowed to slits. "Okay, now you listen to me. You bulldoze your way in here to tell me all these things you've read in the diary—which, by the way, we're not even gonna discuss the fact that you made a copy and kept it without asking—"

"There's no law against that."

He cocked his head. "Tampering with evidence?"

"Can't be evidence if it's a closed, solved case."

Chief Killen sniffed hard, inhaling so that his chest fully expanded before exhaling a deep, impatient sigh. "I said we aren't going to discuss it. Now, that file I gave you, that was supposed to help you get closure, not help you reopen this whole thing. I'm gonna need that back. Now." He held his thick hand out expectantly.

"I don't have it with me." It wasn't a lie. It was locked in the trunk of her car.

He dropped his hand. "Then get it to me as soon as you can."

"How can they just let it go like this? They aren't going to do anything? What about Dr. Beecher? His lawyer?"

"They don't have to do anything because it isn't exculpatory. All it does is mention other people in her life—basically a teenager and some other potential troublemaker who was probably one too, some kid cheating on his girlfriend or something. Just a bunch of high school drama. It doesn't say either of them tried to kill her, or that 'if I end up dead, so-and-so did it.' It doesn't prove that Dr. Beecher didn't do it, or say he was out of town that day or erase all the hard evidence that got Beecher convicted in the first place—fingerprints, soil samples, eyewitness testimony—"

"But if the jury had heard—"

"But they didn't."

"So now what? It's just over?"

"Dani, it's been over. For a long, long time. Just not for you."

"What about the diary? What'll they do with it?"

"It'll go back to Jennifer's parents eventually. I doubt the D.A.'s office will keep it long."

Hard determination steeled in Dani. "This isn't right. It isn't fair."

Chief Killen softened. "I know you think that, but you're wrong. Justice was served. The law was upheld. You know how this works better than anybody."

"Yeah, I think that's the problem," she said, shooting out of her chair so that it almost fell over as she stomped to the door, her back to the Chief.

"I'm gonna need that file back." His words were gentle, but firm. Dani stopped with her hand on the knob for just a moment, then twisted it open without responding and stepped through.

"And don't do anything stupid with that copy *that doesn't exist*, you hear me? I mean—"

But she didn't hear the rest, his words drowned out by the door slamming behind her.

"Boston?"

Dani stopped mid-stride, jerking her head to the right to see Chris Newton coming from the breakroom, holding a muffin in one hand and a "Jerry's Body Shop" mug in the other. She glared at him silently.

"Whoa," he said, and walked tentatively to her, his eyebrows rising, forming tiny lines across his forehead. "You look like you're ready to kill someone."

"Not funny." She knew she had no excuse to be short with him, but she was just so angry, she couldn't help it. Keeping her temper in check wasn't really her strong suit. It wasn't always fair, but when she got riled up, it just sort of...bubbled over... onto everyone around her. It was one of the things she disliked most about herself, and a heady guilt immediately set in.

Instead of backing off, or looking offended, his face scrunched up, a hint of amusement behind his eyes. "Not trying to be funny. Just making an observation. I am a detective, after all. I'm trained to spot people out for blood." Then something shifted, his countenance darkening. "Wait, did something happen last night after I left? Did someone come back to your house?"

"What? No, nothing like that." His concern melted her obstinance and giving in, her shoulders slumped. "They decided not to do anything with the diary. And the Chief confirmed there wasn't any physical evidence in the shed at all."

Chris grimaced. "That's what we heard back this morning. Sorry, Boston. I know you wanted this to turn out differently."

A familiar fire kindled in her belly. "It's just that they're wrong. They are so wrong. The diary mentions other people who could have been involved, who could have had a reason to want Jennifer dead. And they're just going to let it go."

His eyes widened. "Other people? Really?" He pulled her over to his desk and lowered his voice. "What other people?"

He listened intently as she explained.

"Uh, huh. You know," he said, walking over to a chair and dragging it to a spot beside his. He motioned for her to sit, and he followed suit. "You told me that you didn't get all the way through the diary. So, the first thing I have to ask is how you managed to read the rest of it, given that it's still sitting in the D.A.'s office?"

"You can ask a question, Detective, but I can choose not to answer."

A bit of a grin peeked out from the corner of his mouth, but he reined it in quickly. "So, the information in the diary—the prosecution really believes it's not exculpatory?"

She nodded. "They don't see that they have any obligation to hand it over to Dr. Beecher or to reopen the case on their own. They're just giving the diary back to Jennifer's parents."

Chris's charcoal eyes held Dani's for several moments, as if he were mulling something over. Then he gently grasped her forearm and a thread of electricity coursed through Dani.

"Come on, I'll walk you out," he said, rising in tandem with her and walking by her side to the exit, through the lobby, then out the front door.

Even this early in the morning, the air in the parking lot was thick with moisture, promising another grueling day of temperatures forecasted to be near one hundred degrees. Chris veered off to the left, leading her down the sidewalk a good bit, away from the door and out of earshot of anyone who might come in or out.

"Obviously, I wasn't around when all this went down years ago," he said, "but there are still people here who worked that case."

"And?"

"And I got the distinct feeling yesterday that those people do not want this case reopened. Period. No matter what that diary says."

"What people?"

His eyebrows rose.

"Chief Killen?" she ventured, disbelief in her voice. "No, no way."

"He was one of the investigators on the case."

"So?"

"So, he wouldn't want to find out thirteen years later that he missed something which could've kept an innocent man out of jail. Can you imagine the fallout? The embarrassment?" Chris prompted.

Doubt wriggled in her stomach as she considered the effect that outcome would have on the Chief. But it only lasted a second. "No. He wouldn't do that."

"You know the current district attorney was the prosecutor in that case too?"

"Are you suggesting they're conspiring to keep this quiet?"

He shook his head. "Conspiring is too strong a word. I'm suggesting that these people have personal reasons for wanting this case to stay closed, no matter what's in that diary. And since it seems like there's nothing in the diary that definitively clears Beecher anyway, it makes it easy to justify a decision to leave things as they are."

Though he was doing a thorough job of explaining the reasons behind the D.A.'s decision, he wasn't doing much to give her hope. "What's your point?" she asked.

He leaned in, inclining his forehead toward hers. "My point is that I think you've run up against a brick wall. I think you've done all a person could do to try to make sure the right thing was done here—and maybe it's time to leave it now."

He was so close that she could see minuscule flecks of grey in his deep, dark irises and the beginnings of whiskers on his jawline where his shave hadn't been quite close enough.

"Well, thanks for the words of wisdom," she said, stepping back.

He grasped her arm again, his fingers warm on her skin. "But I also wanted to tell you that from where I'm standing, I see it the same way you do. It doesn't seem quite fair. And if there's anything I can do to help, anything I can...smooth over or grease...I will. You just have to ask."

His overture caught her off-guard. There was an earnestness in his tone that made it clear he wasn't just giving her a line. He wasn't just trying to connect or...flirt with her. He meant it. The intensity rippling off him was palpable, and Dani believed that if she had asked him to help her do what she was going to do next, he would have, without question.

But she wouldn't do that to him. She wouldn't put him in that position.

"Thanks, Chris. Really. It's nice to know someone in there is on my side. Even if there's nothing else to be done."

They stood there for a moment, the space between them both slightly awkward and charged, until finally she stepped toward her car, wobbling a bit as her foot dropped off the sidewalk onto the pavement.

"I, um, probably should go. Lots to do today," she said as she backed away, swinging her arms out and in, her hands meeting in a soft clap.

"Oh, right. The reunion," he said.

*Oh, right, the reunion!* She held her face steady, hoping to hide any indication that the reunion was not the errand she had been thinking about. "Yeah, gotta go help Sasha," she agreed, leaking a bit of extra cheer into her voice. "So, I'll, uh, see you around?" she asked, side-stepping farther into the lot.

"By the way," he called as she went, "I'm sending those extra patrols around your house. I know what you said, but better safe than sorry. I just didn't want you to be surprised if you saw them."

Normally, she would have been perturbed by his overriding her insistence that she didn't need the extra protection. Normally, a man ignoring her assessment of a situation—especially her assessment of a security situation as an experienced, knowledgeable police officer—and replacing it with his own would have made her ten shades of angry. But it didn't, which greatly surprised her.

"Fine," she replied, trying to sound at least a little annoyed as she opened her driver's side door. "But I still say I don't need them."

"Yeah, yeah," Chris said indulgently, then tossed her a little wave before heading back inside.

Dani watched him go, then dropped into the driver's seat. She exhaled a cleansing breath in an effort to dispel her lingering anger over the state of things, then started the car, redirecting her focus to her next stop, which had absolutely nothing to do with the Skye High Class of '98 Reunion.

# 10

The regular visitation room at Trenbow Prison, forty miles south of Skye, just off Highway 344, was exactly what one would expect based on television and movies: a long, narrow room, with a plexiglass partition, and handsets on either side to allow the visitor and prisoner to communicate with some semblance of privacy, though all the conversations were recorded for security purposes. At the moment, Dani was the only visitor. Her hard plastic chair was probably older than she was. She had only been sitting in it for ten minutes, and her back was already talking to her. That was on top of the mild headache from the overpowering smell of chemical cleansers permeating the room, layered over something stale and fetid, as if someone had sprayed a ridiculous amount of disinfectant around, but had not actually cleaned anything.

Had this been a scheduled visit on a preset visitation day, Dani would have been able to see him in the larger community visitation room with tables and chairs and no glass, with all the other family and friends who were visiting loved ones. Then there could be hugs and hand squeezes and human connection to remind him that he was not all alone in this world. That he had not been forgotten. At least not by her. But it wasn't a scheduled visit. It was an impulsive, spit-in-the-face-of-propriety move that meant she would be stuck with this partitioned room.

The gums in her mouth hummed, vibrating the way they did whenever she was truly anxious. Seeing him always brought so much back: the terror, the grief, the shock, the guilt, the sadness, the anger—but she endured it, because it was worth it. Especially this time.

After several minutes, he finally stepped through the steel door at the rear dressed in the standard-issue orange uniform of the prison. He made his way to the cubicle opposite her, pulled out the plastic chair and sat, a warm smile on his face as he laid the alligator-clipped stack of copies on the counter in front of him. He lifted the handset on his side. "Hey there, Danielle," he said, his deep voice a bit buzzy as it came through the earpiece. "How are you?"

Dr. Beecher never called her by her nickname. With him it had always been "Danielle," even though her own family called her "Dani." Her heart melted just looking at him—this man who had been like a second father to her. Her own father had been wonderful, but because he was paid by the hour at the garage, there had been a lot of hours he was gone. Dr. Beecher had stood in the gap.

A quick appraisal revealed he had put on a little weight, stretching the uniform a bit, and his salt-and-pepper hair was longer than she remembered. Not too long, just less like a crew cut than before. His round face was as kind as ever, but there was something different about his light brown eyes. Today, instead of the dim, resigned version, they were alight, brimming with hope.

She lifted her handset, feeling a smile crease her face. "Hi, Doc." She never had been able to bring herself to use his first name, despite his insistence. "You look really good," she commented. "Things must be better than they were in March." In fact, she couldn't remember him ever looking this well.

"You could say that. But how are you? How are you doing with packing up the house?"

She had told him on her last visit that she would be back in July to deal with the estate. Leave it to him to ask about that first, before anything else, even with Jennifer's diary sitting in front of him.

"I'm fine. It's...going well, I guess. But I came here to talk about that," she said, pointing to the stack of papers in front of him.

He tapped the top page with two fingers. "I can't believe it. Jennifer's diary."

"I know!" She could hear the excitement in her voice, and resolved to take it down a notch. She didn't want to get his hopes up too high. Adopting a calmer tone, she explained how she found the diary. "I'm sorry I couldn't bring it before now and I know they just gave it to you back there, but, I've read it through and, Doc, I think it might help you." She gave him a quick run-down, hitting the highlights about the secret boyfriend and "creep."

Dr. Beecher rubbed his hands over his face, then exhaled hard, blowing out so that his cheeks expanded. "Have the authorities seen it?"

"Yeah. But they aren't doing much with it. From what the Chief's told me, they don't think it helps you—it's not exculpatory—and they aren't reopening the case. They weren't even going to give you a copy, but I wasn't going to let that happen. I'm the one who found it. They don't get to decide who I give it to."

"Oh, Danielle. You could get in trouble—"

She held up a hand. "You let me worry about that. I don't work for them. It was my call. And I think you and your lawyer should start looking into this boyfriend and this other person with this secret who may have started stalking Jennifer. One of them could be the person that really did this."

His eyes softened. "You still believe in me after all these years."

"You know I do. And now there's finally evidence pointing to someone else."

"But if they won't reopen the case—"

"Then your lawyer has to make them. You have to follow these leads and see where they go. Promise me you'll read it, and that you'll get it to your lawyer—I can do that for you if you want. I can take a copy to him—"

"No. No, to review it he'll just charge me money I don't have. I'm nearly broke. The appeals exhausted most of my savings. I'll read it through. If it's got something in it worth pursuing I promise I'll get it to him myself. Either way," he leaned his head toward the plexiglass, his hand wrapped around the receiver, "it's time you let this go. Make peace with it. I have."

"Let it go? When we've finally found something—"

"You say I look better than you remember? Well, I am better. I mean, I still don't want to be here and if this," he patted the stack of paper, "is my ticket out, I'll take it. Gladly. But if not, I've made my peace with where I am."

"Doc, you're innocent and you've been locked up for thirteen years. How do you make peace with that?"

"Because I finally realized something."

"What?"

"God has me here for a reason."

Dani shifted back in her chair. This was new. She had never heard Dr. Beecher talk about God before. Or anything religious, for that matter. "What do you mean, 'God has you here for a reason'?"

Dr. Beecher leaned his elbows on the narrow tabletop

before him and clasped his hands together, lacing his fingers as he pressed the mouthpiece to his lips.

"Two days after you visited in March, I got a new cellmate. Mac. He's been in the system for thirty-seven years and he's one of the few who actually admits to being guilty of what he was convicted of—robbing a liquor store. He was just eighteen when it happened, and he was so wasted when he did it that he walked out of that store with ninety-eight dollars from the register, never realizing he had shot and killed the clerk in the process."

"Good grief."

"Yeah. Well, Mac's had to make peace with himself, with life and with God. And let me tell you, he's a different bird. He just overflows with positivity, so much that it nearly drowns you. When he first moved in, I thought he was going to drive me crazy. I finally asked him what he had to be so happy about, being locked up in this place, and boy, did he tell me—wouldn't *stop* telling me. How God has had his hand on his life, has forgiven him, has used him in his plans...I eventually had enough and started scheming about how to get Mac transferred to another block. I was even going to pay someone off to make it happen."

Dani felt her face scrunch up, betraying her distaste. "Did you?" It was hard to imagine Dr. Beecher working the system inside the prison to disadvantage another person.

"No."

"What happened?"

"All I can tell you is that one day, in the middle of Mac's ranting, I found myself wishing that I could have that kind of peace and joy while being stuck in a place like this. I stopped wondering if he was crazy, and started wondering if there was a way to get what he has. And there was."

"Which was what?"

"Jesus." When Dani didn't immediately respond, he smiled. "Now you think *I'm* crazy."

"No," she said. She didn't, truly. It just surprised her to hear him talk like that, after years—more than a decade—of showing no interest in spiritual matters. It was quite a turn-around. But she couldn't deny that there was something... lighter...about him. Along with whatever she had seen in his eyes when he first sat down.

"So now, I want to ask you if you ever think about it, Dani?" he asked.

"What, church?"

"No, not church. God."

Dani sighed, her shoulders tensing. She had been raised in church, but hadn't had much to do with it since that summer. Something about what happened to Jennifer Cartwright and the aftermath had soured her on the idea of God having a plan. Or at least one worth following. "Not anymore, Doc. Not for a long time."

"Well, I hope you do. Everybody needs peace, Dani. Even a tough cop like you."

"Tough detective, now," she corrected, allowing herself a small smile.

He beamed. "Really? Oh, that's great. Congratulations."

"Thanks. But I don't want to talk about me. I want to talk about getting you out of here."

He sat up straighter, and sucked in a breath, squaring his shoulders. "Okay, then. Tell me more details about exactly what Jennifer wrote."

For ten minutes Dani walked him through the entries and why she thought the boyfriend and person with the secret —"the creep"—could have been responsible for Jennifer's death.

"Let me ask you," he finally interrupted, "did she write

anything about the hired hand the Pitts were using that summer?"

"No. And Chief Killen brought him up when I talked to him this morning. He said the boyfriend and the stalker she mentioned aren't any different from that migrant worker they looked into. He said none of it changes that all the evidence still points to you. Even though we know you had explanations for all of that."

He tossed her a grateful look. "Yes, I did, but that's neither here nor there now. But the migrant worker...I just thought that, if Jennifer had written something about him, maybe something that implicated him in some way, or at least identified him...I just always thought it was too coincidental that he left so close to her death."

"Did Jennifer ever interact with him?" Dani asked.

"Not that I know of. If she did, she never said anything to me. And you know I never met him."

"But *you* saw him?"

"From a distance a few times, but that was it," Dr. Beecher replied. "Mr. Pitts was insistent that the man was skittish and wanted to be left alone."

"Yeah. I read in the file that the Pitts told the police he wanted to keep to himself. The notes say the Pitts were trying to give him a helping hand by providing him with work over the summer, but he only stayed for about a month. That was it. There wasn't much else about him in there."

Dr. Beecher's eyebrows drew together. "The file?"

She offered him a guilty smile. "Chief Killen let me peruse their file on your case, but not officially, so you should probably keep that information to yourself."

A hint of shadow eclipsed his face. "You're risking too much for me. I don't want you creating problems for yourself."

"Read the diary," she said, ignoring his protests. "Maybe you'll see something I didn't. About the migrant worker, the boyfriend, maybe even this creepy stalker person. Maybe even something that undermines the evidence they have against you."

"Maybe."

"Keep the faith, Doc."

He put a hand to the window and she matched it. "Don't worry," he said. "I will."

## 11

I t was past noon by the time Dani got home from Trenbow Prison, and though part of her wanted to get right into the boxing, she knew that without a break she would never be able to endure the marathon decorating session Sasha had committed her to that evening. So, she forced herself to sit for a few minutes and enjoy the barbecue and slaw sandwich, Coke, and signature tangy potato salad she had picked up from Pepper's BBQ on the way home. But rather than energize her, the surfeit of food left her yearning for a nap.

*I'll just lie down for a minute.*

She tossed the paper remnants of lunch in the trash and dropped hard onto the couch, curling up into a ball. The midday sunlight streamed through the front window, illuminating an army of suspended dust particles before falling across Dani's body like a toasty electric blanket—a cozy contrast to the chilled air-conditioned air. She was out in three minutes.

When she stirred an hour later, she saw that it was two o'clock, and though her drowsy, heavy body would have relished staying exactly where she was, it was time to get some work done. Rubbing the sleep from her eyes, she looked around the room, her stomach sinking. There was still so much to be done. Pushing herself up she started in, filling box after box marked "Sell," "Donate," "Toss," and "Me." After working for a little while she noticed how much more quickly the other boxes—the ones not marked "Me"—were filling up. Her heart winced. It was hard to think of so many of her parents' things being given away or sold for a fraction of what they were worth.

*But I can't take it all. I don't have a choice.*

So, into the "Toss" boxes went the magazines, random instruction booklets and electronics cords buried in the cabinets. The "Donate" boxes got the DVDs—although she did grab a few of the Christmas favorites they had watched year after year—along with flower arrangements, couch pillows and throws. She cleared her dad's books from the entertainment center, packing most of them up in the "Donate" boxes too, except for several she knew to be his favorites—a non-fiction account of a pilot's experiences in World War II, and a three-book series of Westerns that had belonged to her grandfather.

As she deposited those books into a "Me" box, it occurred to her that there were two books even more precious to her mother and father. Marching straight into their master bedroom, she found them exactly where she knew they would be. One worn, thick Bible covered in black leather on her father's nightstand, and one equally worn, thinner Bible, encased in flower-patterned fabric on her mother's nightstand. She reached for her father's first. He had read this, held this, prayed with this so many times, that when her fingers made contact, it was almost as if she were holding his hand once more. She choked back a sob, walked around the bed and gently lifted her mother's Bible, the same sensation overcoming her. She returned to the living room, gently deposited them side by side into a "Me" box, and continued working.

"I can't believe you went to that prison by yourself again," Sasha said from atop the ladder, as she wove white lights into one of the plastic ficus trees scattered throughout the main event room of the Skye Civic Center. "One of us would have gone with you."

"It's not a big deal," Dani said. She stood below Sasha, feeding her the string of lights as Sasha wound them through the limbs.

"I know, but, still."

"I couldn't not go. Not after what was in that diary. Not after the Chief said the prosecution is dropping it."

Sasha made her way down the ladder. "And you think Dr. Beecher's lawyer can really do something with it?"

"He has to try."

The large, open space was a multi-purpose room, the size of a standard gymnasium, with a platform stage at the front. In preparation for the reunion, a dusky brown carpet had been rolled out over the tile, except for the area directly in front of the stage, where a sizable square of faux wood had been laid to serve as a dance floor. Dozens of round, white-linen-covered tables filled the rest of the room, each topped with a vase containing white carnations and greenery, wrapped with a royal-blue ribbon, representing the white and blue of Skye High. Silver-glittered foam numbers affixed to plastic stems rose from the center of the arrangements, forming the number "98."

Sasha turned in a circle, scanning the space. "It's really coming together. I think we're close." A few other volunteers were working in the room, unfolding and spacing chairs around the tables, also stringing lights and hanging an enormous "CLASS OF '98" banner across the back of the stage.

Dani checked her watch. It was already six o'clock. "It should be, we've been working for three hours."

"*You've* been here for three hours. I got here at noon," Sasha chided.

"Sash, I'm sorry. I had to go to the prison and I had to pack up—"

Sasha waved a hand. "Don't worry about it. I know I drafted you into this. You've got real things to do at home." She squeezed her friend's shoulder. "How's that coming? I forgot to ask, I got so wrapped up in your tales from prison."

Dani sighed. "It's coming. I finished the living room. Hopefully I can finish a couple of the other rooms before the reunion tomorrow."

"Looks good!" a familiar male voice sounded from behind them, and Dani turned to see Peter walking in through the main doors at the back, a jovial grin on his face. "I finished up at work and thought I'd come check it out. See if you needed any help." The Skye Youth Center where Peter worked as director was in the same municipal complex, in a building adjacent to the civic center.

A skeptical look crossed Sasha's face as he neared them. "Funny that you made it here just in time to watch us finish."

Peter's face contorted in obviously feigned offense. "Well, I was working all day—"

"Uh, huh—" Sasha droned.

"And besides, it doesn't look like you needed me. It looks great in here."

"It really does, babe. Amazing!" Willett Mason's voice boomed through the space, deeper and louder than Peter's. He had someone in tow, and as they wove their way toward them through the tables, Sasha's eyes flashed to Dani, wide with expectation.

*Chris Newton.* Dani's stomach dropped, embarrassment

rolling through her at the undisguised glee on Sasha's face. She prayed her own face hadn't turned red.

"I kicked off a little early to see if you needed help," Willett said, "and Chris, here, happened to be at the Grille when I mentioned I was on my way over."

"I thought I could maybe lend a hand—if you needed an extra one," Chris said, a bit hesitantly.

Willett eyed him conspiratorially. "Well, I did bribe him. The man was getting takeout to eat by himself at home, and I said that if he wanted to come by here first, we could feed him a proper meal with good company. Of course," he hedged, "it's still takeout from the Grille."

Dani felt her neck grow hot as she watched Sasha turn an electric smile on Chris. "Absolutely. And, we could use a little muscle." She pointed toward the stage. "There's several boxes over there that need to be moved into the storage area behind the stage until it's time to clean all this up. If you men can handle that, it would be a huge help."

"Done and done," Willett said, motioning for Peter and Chris to follow. As they went, Chris looked over his shoulder to cast a fleeting, questioning glance in Dani's direction before facing forward again.

Dani and Sasha watched the men's backs as they went. "Did you do this?" Dani hissed quietly.

"I swear, I had nothing to do with it. And if you want me to undo it, I can make an excuse or something," Sasha whispered.

"And make me look like the bad guy?"

"You won't look like anything. But," Sasha grinned, leveling a pointed gaze at Dani, "it seems like an awful waste to uninvite him at this point. Not to mention rude."

Dani expelled a weary breath.

Sasha tilted her head imploringly. "Look, Peter and Amy are already coming. It won't be like a date or anything."

Dani's eyes narrowed. "And you won't do something stupid or embarrassing to shove us together, like leaving me alone with him while the rest of you get 'caught up' doing something else?"

Sasha solemnly drew an "X" over her heart with her forefinger.

## 12

"I think we're the victims of a sinister plot," Chris whispered, inclining his head toward Dani, who was seated on the bench next to him at the table on Sasha's back porch. The rest of the group had already followed Sasha inside, carrying the last of the plates into the kitchen, ending with Willett closing the sliding glass door with a soft click after he passed through.

"I think you might be right," Dani grumbled, the muted sounds of dishes clanking inside mixing with the summer night song of the crickets. At just after eight o'clock, the last of the gold, orange and pink rays of the sun had set, ushering in the dim dusk. "Sorry about that."

Chris shook his head. "Don't worry about it. It's not like I didn't have my suspicions. Willett was asking a lot of questions about the time you and I spent together at the shed. I figured it was a setup, but I didn't mind." He raised his glass and took a swig of sweet tea.

"You didn't?"

"There's worse ways to spend an evening." He lifted a forefinger from the glass, and pointed it toward the door as a peal of laughter sounded from inside. "They all seem to really love you."

Dani nodded. "We're family. It's mutual."

Though still in the same positions they had occupied during dinner, now, with everyone else gone, Dani became acutely aware of his proximity. She could see the faint freckles on his nose and the length of his eyelashes. She fidgeted, smoothing her capris and trying to inconspicuously scoot a little more toward the other end of the bench. Chris responded by fully twisting toward her and propping an elbow onto the table, resting his cheek in his hand.

"They also seem pretty worried about you and your involvement with the Cartwright case and that Dr. Beecher."

"I don't know about worried. Honestly, they're probably just tired of it. Ready for me to move on," Dani said. A pang of guilt struck as she realized that, once again, most of their dinner had been consumed with the details of her day—her visits with the Chief and Dr. Beecher, and what she had uncovered in the diary.

"They're the ones that brought it up tonight. And they sure asked you a lot of questions for people who are tired of hearing about it." Chris pursed his lips, looking thoughtful. "And for what it's worth, I don't blame you for taking the copy of the diary out to Dr. Beecher."

"You don't?"

He lifted his head from his hand and shook it. "If it could help the guy, why shouldn't he see it? If he's really innocent, it might be his last chance."

"Exactly. What harm could it do?" But as she said it, and took in his dark eyes watching her intently, she remembered who he was and where he worked, the thought sending a nervous flare through her. "I, um, wasn't planning on bothering the Chief with all that, though. About seeing Dr. Beecher at the prison."

"I imagine not."

"But, now that you know, are you going to tell him?"

He shrugged. "I don't see why I need to. It's not my case. Not anymore, since they decided not to reopen it."

Dani felt the corner of her mouth turn up.

"Besides," Chris continued, "if Beecher or his attorney do anything with that copy, the Chief'll find out soon enough."

"He won't be happy you didn't say anything."

"Well, I'm not going to tell him that I knew. Are you?" he asked, his eyebrows rising.

Dani rolled her lips inward, sealing her mouth shut, and shook her head.

"So, there you go." He poured more tea into his glass and looked questioningly at her with the pitcher raised.

"No, thanks," she said. She couldn't deny that there was a certain something about him that intrigued her. The breeze picked up again and she caught the scent of cloves coming off his skin. It was becoming clear why Sasha and Amy had labeled him the town's most eligible bachelor.

"What's next for you?" he said.

"What? You mean tonight?"

"Just in general. I know the reunion is tomorrow."

*Right, the reunion. The reunion I don't have a date for. The reunion I'm going to walk into alone.*

"Oh, tomorrow's a full packing day. I'm going to try to do a few more rooms before the reunion. Then once that's over, I can really focus on finishing it up before I leave on Thursday."

"You sure you can't use a hand?"

*Could she?* She paused longer than she meant to before answering. "No, really. Thanks."

"Well, call if you need boxes moved or whatever."

"I've got friends here that have been bugging me to do just that since I arrived. I'm covered, really."

"And I'm not a friend?"

Dani chuckled at first, thinking he was flirting again, but quickly broke off when she caught the surprising and somewhat disproportionately hurt look on his face.

"Um, sure you are," she said, trying to smooth it over. "I'm just saying I'm not going to take advantage of a new friend when the ones who have owed me for decades are available."

"It's not taking advantage if—"

The porch door slid open and Sasha stuck her head out. "You guys doing okay out here? We're digging into the ice cream. Peach today—it's really good."

Chris slid off the bench and stood. "I've had enough of Willett's homemade ice cream at the Grille to know that you don't want to miss it, and that it doesn't last long. You'd better move fast," he said, eyeing Dani teasingly before slipping inside the door, leaving her alone on the bench, wondering what in the world had just happened.

## 13

Chris left Sasha's before anyone else, giving Dani the opportunity to read Sasha and Willett the riot act for trying to throw her and Chris together after explicitly promising not to. They both protested despite the obvious porch abandonment, with Peter and Amy giggling off in the corner about it until Dani turned on them, accusing them of being co-conspirators. But in truth, her righteous indignation was only shelled out half-heartedly. She hadn't minded being on the porch alone with Chris. Hadn't minded it one bit. Other than the odd little exchange at the end where he seemed to get his feelings hurt, they had gotten on really well. And she had probably misread that anyway.

Thoughts of their conversation and the way his mouth was a little crooked when he smiled were still rolling through her brain as she pulled into her driveway well after nine thirty. But when she turned the car off, reality set in and she put the brakes on her reminiscing. *This is ridiculous*, she thought, practicality beating out romanticism as she made her way to her door, her arms laden with the leftovers Sasha had insisted she take with her.

*Spending any time at all thinking about Chris Newton is abso-lutely pointless. What are you going to do? Date him long distance from Boston?*

"You're being an idiot," she said aloud to no one, as she inserted the key into the garage's side door lock, then froze.

The hair she had plucked from her own head before leaving earlier, then wedged between the frame and the door upon shutting it, was gone. Her makeshift trespass warning had been triggered.

Someone had been there.

Though her senses hummed, a calm borne of her training settled through Dani as she set the leftovers down, unlocked the door and pushed it open with a long, drawn-out squeak. The weak, motion-sensor light of the overhead garage door unit flicked on and she stepped inside, her pistol drawn. She had been carrying it with her since the scare of the other night, just in case.

It was quiet inside the garage. She squatted down to look underneath the only vehicle in it, her mother's Honda Accord. Nothing.

Using her free hand, she unlocked the interior door leading to the kitchen and pushed it open. The house was also quiet, with only the hum of the refrigerator droning away. The light from a lamp she had left on in the living room spilled through into the kitchen, bathing the room in a soft glow. Everything seemed to be in place.

Flicking on the overhead lights as she went, she moved room to room until she completed a sweep of the entire house. Unlike the intrusion of the day before, this time there were no odd, little suggestions that tampering had occurred. As far as she could tell, whoever had been here—and someone had defi-nitely been there because that hair did not remove itself—had simply entered...and then what?

*And why?*

They weren't stealing. They weren't vandalizing. They hadn't been squatting here, as Chris had suggested. Dani had checked with the property manager who insisted there had been no indication of a break-in since March. There was only one thing that had changed.

*Me.*

Whoever was doing this was interested in her. In her, or in what she was doing there. But it was hard to imagine she had attracted a personal stalker at some point between arriving in Skye a few days ago and the first break-in. That just didn't seem plausible. Nor did the idea that anyone cared enough about the settlement of her parents' estate to break in to learn more. No, there was really only one possibility that made sense.

Someone was deeply interested in her investigation into Jennifer's murder.

Or afraid of it.

HALF AN HOUR LATER, Dani settled into her father's recliner with a cup of cocoa in hand, her mind spinning, analyzing the possibilities. Cocoa on a hot July night in Alabama was an odd choice, granted, but there was something comforting and calming about the chocolatey concoction, and she sipped it slowly as she thought.

*Who would even know I've been looking into Jennifer's murder again?*

It only took a second to realize those prospects were endless. She had been seen going in and out of the police station. It was a small town and her obsession with the case and Dr. Beecher's innocence was general knowledge—at least among the people who had been around back then. People liked to talk. Assumptions would probably have been made.

*But the diary? Who would know about that?*

That list was long too. Everyone at the station would know by now, as well as anyone they had gossiped to—a spouse or girlfriend or boyfriend and so on. For that matter, if Chris and Willett had been talking about her at the Grille, it was possible that mention of the diary, or at least her renewed interest in the case, slipped out then, and could have been overheard by any number of busybodies. And then there was everyone in the D.A.'s office...

Frustrated, and wanting answers she couldn't divine, she reached for the case file and set it on her lap, running a hand over the typed label on the front that read, "Homicide. Cartwright, Jennifer. 7/8/1995." The word "SOLVED" in large, red letters was scrawled diagonally beneath the label. A twinge of guilt pricked her over the fact that she still *had* the file, but not enough to make her put it down.

She glanced at her copy of Jennifer's diary on the coffee table. Certain that the key to figuring this all out lay somewhere within or between the diary and file, she set the empty mug on a side table, crawled onto the floor and began spreading the documents out, sorting by date, relevance and connection. She was going to take it all apart, compare everything, sift through every fact and detail—present or missing—and find something that would break the case open. Because something had to be there.

It just had to.

# 14

P rimary report. Scene report. Witness statements. Inventory of evidence. Autopsy report...

The file contained nothing new. She had heard it all before, read it all before—for goodness' sake, part of it had come directly from her.

The primary report listed the victim as Jennifer Joan Cartwright, homicide, found July 9, 1995. Date of death July 8, 1995. She was fifteen. There was a physical description that matched what Dani remembered from that day: blond, blue eyes, medium-length hair, denim shorts, white top, Skechers. Clothes spattered with blood. Apparent blunt force trauma to the head, later confirmed by the coroner.

There were photos of the scene and a report with a diagram, marking where Jennifer's body had been found, and measurements giving its distance from the riverbank, gravel road, fence, etcetera. Blood spatter just feet away from the body evidencing the likely scene of the murder was indicated on the diagram, as well as a few other random blood deposits in the area. There was also a notation that Jennifer's bicycle had been found on the other side of the barbed-wire fence, several yards down the riverbank toward the water, as if someone had tossed it over in an effort to hide it. They had taken fingerprints from the bicycle and dusted the shed, even though there was no indication any part of the crime had occurred there. But from what Dani remembered, nothing useful had come from either—just Jennifer's prints on the bike and the Pitts' prints and dozens of partials with no matches from the shed, likely from all the adults and kids in and out of it over the years. They had even eventually tried to get prints from the room over the Pitts' garage where the migrant worker had stayed, but by then weeks had gone by and Mrs. Pitts had already given it a good scrubbing.

Dani found her own name at the top of the first witness statement. *Danielle Lake. 15 yrs old. 1108 Applegate Lane, Skye, AL. 205-555-1777.* The paper was smooth to the touch as she passed her fingers over the words, written by the officer who had interviewed her. She still remembered sitting in the small room at the station, wrapped in a blanket, shaking, her parents on either side of her as she recounted the horrible experience. She couldn't remember the officer's name, but according to the report, it was Officer Jim Weston.

*Funny that I don't even remember his name or what he looked like, when I can remember every agonizing detail about Jennifer.*

But what she did recall about the interview with Officer Weston with stark accuracy was the cold metal table she sat behind and stared at continuously because she was too afraid to look up at him, and the frantic scratching of his pen against paper, as he scribbled notes while she spoke. Of course, the interview had been recorded too, though the tape wasn't in this copy of the file. But Officer Weston seemed to have gotten a thorough account down by hand—from the beckoning honeysuckle bush to her coveting Jennifer's Skechers.

Then there was the autopsy report, with all its gory details. There were only two things it mentioned that Dani had not seen herself when she discovered Jennifer: the blunt force trauma to the back of Jennifer's head; and that a one-inch wide, three-inch long section of Jennifer's hair had been cut from the back, leaving jagged ends, as if someone had inefficiently sawed it off.

The police had kept the bit about the hair under wraps, so that Dani only first learned about it during the trial. Dr. Beecher's attorney had argued that the fact that the hair had never been recovered—and certainly had not been found in Dr. Beecher's possession—was evidence of his innocence and that another person was the murderer. But it hadn't worked. The jury was apparently more convinced of his guilt by the finding of Jennifer's bracelet in Dr. Beecher's nightstand. It hadn't mattered that the other piece of jewelry missing from Jennifer —the twisted-vines ring which the diary now explained had been given to her by a secret boyfriend—had never been found either, which Dr. Beecher's lawyer also argued pointed to another person.

According to the notes from Jennifer's parents' interviews, they thought she was spending the night of July 8th with Kendall—Kendall only lived a five-minute bike ride away—so they didn't think anything about it when Jennifer didn't come home the next morning. According to Kendall's interview, she apparently knew nothing about that, but said that it wasn't unusual for Jennifer to just show up and spend the night, so maybe that's what Jennifer had planned on doing and just didn't get a chance to ask Kendall before she was killed.

Jennifer's parents also told the police the twisted-vines ring was something Jennifer had purchased for herself several weeks before her death at a little craft market in town. From the diary, Dani knew that wasn't true, and soon Jennifer's parents would know it too. Her heart ached at the thought of Jennifer's parents learning that their daughter had lied to them about the ring, and apparently so much else. The realization that they had not known their child as well as they thought they did would certainly sting, would still cut to the bone even after all this time. Not to mention how hard it would be to learn that their daughter had been afraid to tell them about the person she had come to love for fear of their disapproval.

*Will her parents make the connection that, if Jennifer had trusted them more, that if they had known these things about her, they would have had someone to point the police to?*

Of course they would, and Dani knew the guilt of that would weigh heavily. Would it make them doubt what they had maintained all along? The Cartwrights had always been staunch believers in Dr. Beecher's guilt, actively seeking his conviction. Now what would they think with a boyfriend, secrets and a potential stalker in the mix during Jennifer's last days?

The one thing that Dr. Beecher's conviction had brought the Cartwrights was closure. Now, the unearthing of the diary would undo that as well. Initially, Dani had thought that returning Jennifer's diary to them would be like giving them back a small piece of their daughter. But now, she realized it might actually achieve the opposite, taking even more of Jennifer away as they were forced to accept that they hadn't truly known her.

*Pain. So much pain surrounding this tragedy. Pain that was seemingly never going to end.*

A swell of righteous anger rose within Dani, her hands clenching the pages of the copied diary harder, the sheets crinkling beneath her grasp as she thought of the person responsible.

The person who had murdered Jennifer Cartwright and gotten away with it.

The person who had robbed her dear friend of his family, reputation and freedom.

The person who had been her singular obsession for the past thirteen years.

The person she was going to nail.

## 15

D ani spent the night scouring the documents to no avail. She finally went to bed at three in the morning, frustrated, her sleep plagued by the crushing weight of the realizations she'd had the night before. After a rough two hours of sleep, she finally gave up, rolled out of bed and flipped open her laptop. If her discovery of this diary was going to cause more pain, it wasn't going to be for nothing.

She drafted a quick email to Larry Holmes, Dr. Beecher's attorney, even though part of her felt she was betraying Dr. Beecher by bypassing him. But what if he decided this wasn't worth pursuing? She couldn't let that happen.

Dani did her best to explain the situation to Mr. Holmes, outlining what she had read in the diary and the potential opportunities she believed those revelations presented. She indicated she would be happy to provide him a copy of the diary for his review. There was obviously no way she could mention the case file or offer it to Mr. Holmes without betraying the Chief's trust. But Dani was fairly certain that between the trial, discovery and just general talk, Mr. Holmes was probably already familiar with the information it contained. After reading the email several times, she clicked "Send," slapped the laptop shut and shuffled off to the kitchen to make breakfast. As it was a Saturday, she didn't expect to hear back from him until Monday at the latest, but her heart was a bit lighter for having reached out.

As she whipped up pancakes from the meager groceries she had purchased, she made a plan for the day. The reunion wasn't until six thirty. Until then, she would sort as much of the house as she could. Today she would be moving on to the bedrooms that used to be hers and Nikki's, and if she had time after that, the dining room, bathrooms and linen closet. If she made it through those, it would be a very productive day.

It wasn't lost on her that she was saving the most difficult rooms for last. Her father's office and her parents' bedroom. Difficult, not only in terms of the most belongings in a single space, but also because they were the most personal areas of the house. The most sentimental. The most emotionally racking. Even though she and Nikki weren't close, it would have been nice to have her sister there for that part of the process. Someone to lean on. Someone who understood the loss, because they too had lived it.

But Nikki wasn't there, and although Sasha and Peter had both offered to come help today, she had refused them. Sasha had enough to deal with, being in charge of the reunion, and Peter—well, she didn't really have a good excuse for not letting him help, except that, if her sister couldn't be there, she would just rather do it alone. When the time came to move boxes around, she would take all the help she could get. But the packing was simply too intimate and too heart-wrenching to undertake under the watchful, worried eyes of others.

Dani stabbed the last bite of fluffy, vanilla-laced pancake, wiped up the maple syrup pooling on her plate, and washed it down with the rest of the orange juice in her glass. After depositing the dishes in the dishwasher, she marched off to get ready, resolved to get through at least two rooms before lunch.

IT WAS NEARLY noon before Dani started feeling hungry again. Sitting back on her heels on the floor of her old bedroom, a growing sense of accomplishment filled her. She had stuck to her plan, working relentlessly to get through Nikki's old room first—a fairly easy task given that Nikki had cleared it of anything she wanted when she was there in March.

Dani's own room had proven more difficult, wringing more than one bout of tears from her as she pulled memorabilia from her closet and dresser drawers, long forgotten, but riddled with memories. In this room there were more boxes marked "Me" than in any of the others. After two hours of work, she held the last of it in her hands—a stuffed green frog with a felt crown that had been her childhood favorite, its much-loved fuzz now worn and perpetually flat. She gingerly placed it into the last box and closed the top, patting it as she rose.

She was headed down the hallway, trying to decide what to do about lunch when the doorbell rang. Once again through the peephole, she saw Chris Newton, this time standing there with a grin and a pizza box.

"What are you doing here?" she asked, swinging the door wide.

He shrugged. "You said you'd be working in the house all day. I thought you might be able to use a break. You've got to eat, right?"

Dani gripped the edge of the door, trying to keep her face from reflecting the mild annoyance she felt. It wasn't that she didn't appreciate the gesture, but she had *specifically* turned down Chris's offer of help the night before for good reasons, and thought she had been pretty clear about that. Yet, here he was, intruding on the very activities she had barred even her oldest and dearest friends from sharing with her.

Why the persistence? Had Sasha sent him over? And was he really that interested in her?

*Would I mind if he was?*

She stopped that thought in its tracks, because, once again —Boston vs. Skye. She shifted her weight, glancing at the ground, stalling for a second before meeting his gaze.

"Look, this is...so nice," she said. "But, I really meant what I said last night, Chris. This is something I need to do by myself."

His eyes widened. "Dani, no...I'm not here to help. You were pretty clear about that. I genuinely just figured you might be working too hard to take a lunch break. I didn't know what you had in the house so I brought this for you. I'm not staying." He held the box out to her. "I took a chance. You seemed like a supreme pizza kind of girl—er, woman."

The delicious scent of oven-baked crust, tomato sauce and oregano wafted up from the box, which displayed a Tagalini's Pizza logo, her favorite pizza place in town. Dani's stomach rumbled audibly and she clutched at it.

"Sounds like I wasn't wrong," Chris said with a smirk.

Dani narrowed her eyes. "You took a chance, or has somebody been talking to Sasha?"

He eyed her roguishly. "Are you going to take it or not?" he asked, his timbre dropping.

She tossed him a playful frown, grabbed the box and stepped aside. "Come on in," she said, adding an exaggerated sigh of concession. "I mean, since you went to all this trouble..."

He slid by her and she followed him inside, wondering where this was headed. Wherever that was, one thing was certain.

Sasha was going to get an earful the second he left.

# 16

———

"So, I chased the kid into the alley," Chris said, continuing the story he'd been telling for the last five minutes, "the one by Carrington's Cleaners on Second Avenue—"

"Yeah, I know it," Dani said. They sat across from each other at the kitchen table, the pizza box opened before them, the ice in their tea half melted.

"—and, there's this ten-foot-high chain-link fence at the back and he just runs up and scales the thing."

"Impressive."

"Exactly. So I get there and grab on, figuring he's going to be long gone if I don't follow him over, only, then I see that he isn't running anymore. He's just standing there on the other side, watching me. And he says, 'Ain't no way you get over that before I take off, old man. See you, loser.' And he turns on the speed. Well, there's no way I'm having that—"

"Of course not," Dani said, finishing off her third slice.

"Exactly. So I pull myself up and over, but my jacket gets caught on the top and I lose my grip, fall eight feet and land on my ankle. Broke it. And the little monster's disappeared. For six months I was the guy who got outsmarted by a ten-year-old rolling houses. They actually called me 'Charmin.'"

"Ouch."

"Yeah. Didn't end until another guy got a concussion from a confused little old lady who called 9-1-1 about a break-in, then whacked him in the head with a bat when he showed up to investigate."

"What did they call him?"

Chris grinned wryly. "Mrs. Doubtfire."

"Nice."

"Okay," Chris said, rubbing his hands together, shedding any stray crust crumbs. "Your turn. Your most embarrassing moment on the job."

Dani squeezed her eyes tight and groaned. "All right. First day. Straight out of the academy. I'm in the car with my partner and we're not on patrol for more than ten minutes when this woman comes up to my window at a red light, taps on it and tells us some guy stole her purse just up the block, then ran into a store. My partner pulls over in the only free spot, leaves the keys in—"

"Oh no," Chris interrupted, his face twisting into a pained expression.

"—and tells me to give him a minute and be ready to follow in the car if the guy makes a run for it. He hustles into the store, and I walk around the front of the car to the driver's side—a little slow, right, because I'm watching for him the whole time. Then I hear a door slam. I look and there's some college-aged kid in the driver's seat, with a stupid grin on his face. I'm yelling at him to get out, yanking on the door handle, which he has of course locked. He pulls out of the space and drives away just as my partner walks out of the store, with the perp handcuffed."

"Wow."

"Yeah. They recovered the car just six blocks away, but still. The damage was done."

"How long did it take you to ride that one out?" He grinned smugly. "No pun intended."

"I got a remote-control patrol car from my Secret Santa for four years running."

"Yikes," he said, then popped the last of his crust into his mouth. He chewed for a moment, then swallowed. "How far have you gotten today with the packing?"

"It's coming along."

"Must be hard."

"It is. I'll be glad when it's done." She rose, picking up the pizza box. "You want any more?"

He patted his stomach. "Nope. Couldn't eat another bite."

Dani deposited the box in the fridge while he put the plates in the dishwasher. She turned back before he looked up, and found herself watching the way he moved. Her initial annoyance triggered by his unannounced visit had long evaporated. He was easy to talk to. Funny. And he was a cop, so he understood her on a level that non-cops didn't. Plus, he wasn't doing that thing Sasha and Peter tended to do—watching her uncomfortably closely, looking for signs that she wasn't handling it all well—or at least he didn't seem to be. It was just lunch, pure and simple.

He looked up and caught her staring, at which she awkwardly backpedaled a few steps.

He smiled, but graciously avoided looking too 'cat-that-ate-the-canary' about it. "So, um, don't be too mad at Sasha," he said, leaning against the counter, crossing one ankle over the other.

"About what?" Dani asked, attempting an innocent inflection.

"Oh come on, you know as well as I do that she's matchmaking here."

"So she did tell you to come by! I knew it."

"No, she called and...hinted...that you might forget to eat."

Dani offered him an apologetic smile. "Look, Sash thinks it's her responsibility to see me...involved again. I'm really sorry you got wrapped up in it."

"Well, I'm not," he said evenly.

His forthrightness made her uncomfortable and she snorted softly, deflecting her self-consciousness.

"She just wants you to be happy."

"Yeah. I know she means well—she and Willett, both," Dani said, "but she doesn't have the best track record when it comes to this sort of thing."

"Really?"

"When I was a freshman at Boston College, Sash came to visit over her spring break. She met this guy at a party and was positive he was the one for me. Did her thing, pushed us together."

"What happened?"

"Three years later Finn and I got married."

Chris expelled a throaty laugh. "So, she got it right."

Dani shook her head. "Couldn't have been more wrong. Married at twenty-two, divorced at twenty-six."

"What happened?"

She huffed a tired sigh. The story never got easier to tell. "He decided he wanted something—someone—different. I loved him and he loved her."

"I'm so sorry."

"It was the hardest thing I've ever been through, next to my parents, obviously," she said, waving a hand at the room vaguely. "So, you can understand why I'm reluctant to let Sasha play a guiding role in my love life."

Dani's phone went off, the ring a short recording of the theme from *The Office*. It wasn't a number she recognized.

"Hello?" she answered, and held up a finger to Chris, mouthing the word, *sorry.*

"Is this Danielle Lake?" The voice was deep, male and older.

"Speaking."

"Ms. Lake, this is Larry Holmes, Dr. Thomas Beecher's attorney."

A jolt of electricity zinged her. "Of course! Mr. Holmes! I, um, didn't expect to hear from you until Monday at the earliest."

"Normally, you wouldn't have. But I've received some news that required my attention and when I opened my email to deal with it, I saw your email and thought I should get in touch, seeing as how you and Dr. Beecher were close. He always spoke very highly of you."

"Well, I've always thought a lot of him too. That's why—" She cut herself off as a cold stone slipped into her stomach. "What do you mean 'spoke' highly of me?"

Mr. Holmes paused, clearing his throat. "That's just it, Ms. Lake. Dr. Beecher is dead."

"I CAN'T BELIEVE IT," Dani croaked hoarsely, sitting on the couch with her head in her hands. Chris sat beside her, his eyebrows drawn together as he watched her.

"What exactly did he say?"

"He was stabbed by one of the inmates with some kind of shank." A timid sob escaped her lips as she sucked in a staggered breath. "I just saw him yesterday morning," she said, her voice pleading. "He was doing so well."

"Do they know what happened?"

"Apparently three inmates cornered Dr. Beecher's cellmate after breakfast and started pushing him around pretty hard. Dr. Beecher saw what was happening and tried to intervene. One of them whipped out the shank and—" Her sharp intake of breath cut off her words.

*He's dead. Dr. Beecher is dead. The day after I brought him the diary, he's dead.*

Another gale of nausea assaulted her as she lifted her gaze to meet Chris's. He must have seen the panic in her eyes, because he started shaking his head forcefully.

"No. No, Boston. I know what you're thinking, but, no. You didn't cause this."

"How do we know that? I bring him the diary and less than twenty-four hours later he's dead? That can't be a coincidence!" The desperation in her voice rang in her ears.

"This wasn't directed at Dr. Beecher. You said they were starting in on his cellmate, right?"

She nodded.

"So, he just got in the way. Stepped into the wrong fight. It had nothing to do with you."

Her face was hot and wet and she roughly dragged a hand across her cheeks to wipe away the tears. "I wish I could believe that."

For a moment they sat in silence, Chris apparently at a loss for any other encouragement. "What did his attorney say about the diary? Did they recover it?"

Another pang of sadness struck her. "It's there. They'll send it to his family along with his other belongings, but Mr. Holmes said the diary and whatever might be revealed in it doesn't matter now that Dr. Beecher's dead. There's no one to pay him to pursue it. At best he'd be attempting to clear Dr. Beecher's name. If it had been a matter of getting Dr. Beecher out of jail, he said he would have helped even if Dr. Beecher couldn't pay him. But now, he just doesn't see the point."

"Wouldn't the family pay him?"

"He doesn't think so. It's just the ex-wife and the kids down in Florida. I can't see her paying for it and anything Dr. Beecher will have left the children, *if* he has anything at this point, will likely be held in trust for them. Dr. Beecher told me himself when I saw him that he was essentially broke."

"So, it just ends?"

She nodded and sniffed. "I guess so." She straightened in her chair and dropped her shoulders. "Look, I'm really sorry. I'm not the weepy type. It's just a real blow." She shot up, suddenly feeling a need to be alone again. "Thanks for lunch and everything, but I should probably get back to work."

"Sure, of course," he said, following her to the front door. He walked through as she held it open, turning back toward her when he reached the bottom of the front steps.

"I get how you feel, Boston, but it's really not your fault. It's just an awful coincidence."

Though his words didn't change anything, for his sake, she smiled weakly. "Thanks." He returned the smile, then started down the front path.

A burst of something reckless over and above her grief exploded within her as she watched him go. The feeling surprised her almost as much as what she did next.

"Um, Chris?" she called out.

He paused mid-stride and swiveled back. "Yeah?"

*What am I doing? Have I completely lost my mind? Stop it!*

"Oh, um, I, uh...just thanks."

He nodded. "You already said that. I'll see you later, Boston. Try to have a good reunion."

"You too," she replied, immediately feeling like an idiot.

*"You too?" What is wrong with me?* But if he heard her, he didn't say anything.

He drove off before she managed to do anything else embarrassing, and she went back inside, berating herself.

*I can't believe I nearly asked him to go to the reunion with me.*

It was the grief. And the shock. Had to be.

*Dr. Beecher. Dead. Just like her parents. And Jennifer. And any hope of finding the truth.*

This incredible, unforgivable miscarriage of justice hadn't just taken Dr. Beecher's freedom, it had killed him. And with cruel irony, only one day after he had finally been offered the tiniest sliver of hope.

According to Mr. Holmes, the funeral plans in Dr. Beecher's will allowed for a small service and burial, but that wouldn't take place for a couple of weeks, as his children lived in Florida with their mother and needed time to make travel arrangements. So Dani wouldn't even get to do that small thing to honor him—to be present for his funeral, to say a proper goodbye.

Pushing down a heavy sense of failure, she headed to the dining room, hoping to bury the feeling in busyness.

## 17

The thumping sounds of *Backstreet's Back* filled the civic center's event hall as two hundred-plus people danced, ate, and caught up with old friends. The neon beams projected from the lights on the DJ's table cast alternating hues of pink, green, yellow and blue across the room, giving a club-like feel to the space, while the flickering candles on the tables added a contrasting touch of coziness.

Dani stood off to one side with Sasha and Willett, nursing a glass of white wine and chatting with people she hadn't seen in ten years, many coming over to congratulate Sasha on the evening. Dani wore a simple, fitted black cocktail dress with spaghetti straps, hemmed just above the knee with a little ruffle at the bottom that fluttered as she moved. She smiled and hugged and looked at pictures of children and met spouses, all with a smile on her face that she didn't really feel. The news from earlier had just hit too hard.

On the upside, only a few people asked about Finn. Given that they had been married in Boston, and that Sasha and Peter were the only friends she had invited from home, she wasn't even sure many knew she had been married at all. Dani dismissed the few polite inquiries with a quick, "we aren't together anymore," at which point the person always quickly changed the topic, which was perfectly fine with her.

"I thought the tribute to Jennifer was lovely," said the woman talking to Sasha, who, after a minute of straining, Dani eventually recognized as Ellie Camper, a former Skye Warriors cheerleader.

"We needed to do something," Sasha replied. "It didn't feel right not to."

"Absolutely." Ellie clasped Sasha's arm, her french-tipped nails making indentions in Sasha's skin as she lowered her voice. "I saw on the news that Dr. Beecher was killed in prison." Her mouth turned down, disgust creasing her lips. "Serves him right."

Heat flushed up Dani's neck. Though her divorce hadn't come up much, Dr. Beecher's death had been discussed incessantly, prompted by a sensationalized news report earlier in the day that splashed it all over the airwaves. She had been forced to listen ad nauseam to the steady stream of vicious gossip—in particular the general consensus that Dr. Beecher had it coming—without rising to his defense because she didn't want to make a scene.

She slammed her wine glass down on a table, causing Ellie to jump. "Um, Sash, I'm going to go grab something to eat. I'll be back in a minute," Dani said, and barreled away to the buffet on the opposite side of the room.

Though she hadn't realized she was hungry, her stomach rumbled at the zesty scents greeting her as she neared the long row of tables displaying the sumptuous feast catered by The Skye Grille. Willett had outdone himself, venturing far beyond the Grille's standard offerings to include shrimp skewers and cocktail sauces in three levels of spice, mushroom caps stuffed with goat cheese and rosemary, a variety of salads and sides, and a mouth-watering carving station serving roast beef that seemed to melt at the touch of the knife.

*Maybe I can just stand here and stuff my face for the rest of the night and avoid having to talk to anyone else.*

She filled her plate, and was just looking for an empty bar-height table to hunker down at, when a male voice spoke right behind her left ear, his breath warm on her skin.

"Hungry much?"

She turned to see her high school sweetheart, Bailey King—six foot four, blond as ever, though perhaps a little more filled out than she remembered, but in a good way.

"Bailey! Oh," she exclaimed, and went to hug him, then realized she had the plate in one hand and her drink in the other. After fumbling to set both down on the buffet, she embraced him with a vigorous, though slightly awkward hug.

"High school sweetheart" might have been stretching it a bit. They had only dated four months during her senior year, but it was the longest relationship she ever had in Skye and she had adored him. Even now, her heart did a little flip at the nearness of him, such a surreal thing after so long. The irony was, she was the one who broke up with him, and had only done it out of insecurity. He was popular, a star of the basketball team, and she convinced herself that it was only a matter of time before he dumped her. He had fought her over it, but she hadn't relented. Later, when her feelings didn't fade and she had to watch him go out with other girls, she had kicked herself for being so stupid. He was funny and kind, not one of those high school jocks out to prove something all the time, loved the same kinds of books and movies—even *Titanic*, which he publicly scorned, but secretly loved, taking her to see it no less than eight times. And he had been very easy to look at.

Still was.

For five glorious minutes they conversed about all things not related to Jennifer Cartwright: where they were living—he

was in Providence—what they were doing—he was an investment advisor—and the fact that they were both single.

*He's single.* That surprised her. *"Never found the right woman,"*
*he had said.*

A warm, fuzzy feeling slowly spread out from her center as
their conversation rolled along easily.

*His eyes are greener than I remember.*

"I thought I'd hate it when the company transferred me to
Providence, but I love it," he said.

"I had no idea you'd moved up north. Last I heard you were
in New Orleans."

Those olive eyes narrowed playfully. "Looks like that may
have been an oversight on my part. I'll have to update my
address book."

*That grin.* Dani's stomach flipped again, and the sensation
almost made her laugh. "Um," she said quickly, in an attempt to
suppress the reflex, "maybe it was."

*He was flirting with her.*

*Providence isn't that far from Boston. An hour-and-a-half drive,*
*maybe? It's not out of the realm of possibility.*

Then the hammer fell.

"So, I remember how you were involved in, well...finding
Jennifer Cartwright. I heard about Dr. Beecher today. Killed in
prison—crazy stuff."

Her heart sank. So here it was again. A knot formed in her
chest, hardening as the seconds ticked by. She just couldn't get
away from it. Then the strangest thought occurred to her.

*Maybe I'm not supposed to get away from it. Maybe the fact that*
*it keeps coming up again and again actually means something. Like a*
*sign—a sign that I shouldn't give up too quickly. Am I supposed to*
*keep pressing?*

*Yes,* she thought.

She straightened up, fresh resolve blossoming. Just because
the authorities and Mr. Holmes saw no reason to push any

further, didn't mean she had to give up. She wasn't in it for the money, didn't care about the politics, and the fact that Dr. Beecher was dead didn't mean she couldn't clear his name. That alone would mean so much to his children and give meaning to the price Jennifer's parents were going to pay for the unearthing of her diary.

Not to mention finding the actual murderer.

That thought electrifying her, she looked around the venue and realized she was smack-dab in the center of a room full of potential witnesses. People who had known Jennifer. People Jennifer might have confided in. One of them could even *be* the mysterious boyfriend. Or the stalker.

"I don't think Dr. Beecher killed her," Dani replied starkly, her words firm.

Bailey's forehead wrinkled. "You don't?"

"I never did. I knew Dr. Beecher well, and there's no way he did it." Energized, she plunged in. "In fact, did you know that Jennifer had a boyfriend at the time she died?"

"No, I didn't," he said.

"Are you sure? You guys dated for a while, right?" Her words were coming fast now, all business. The detective in her was taking over.

"Just briefly in our freshman year. Long before you and I did."

"But you never heard about her dating someone during the summer she died?"

"No, I really didn't." He shifted his weight to his back foot, tilting his head as if appraising her anew.

"What about anyone she had a problem with? Someone who might have been paying her too much attention? Stalking her?"

He squinted and something about his stance tensed. "Dani...why all the questions? Are you looking into this? Are the police?"

She pressed her lips together, calculating what to say. She didn't want to overstep and get in trouble with the Chief by implying something that wasn't true, but she needed her involvement to sound legitimate.

"There's...been some new information that's come across my path and I just wanted to follow it up. A room full of people who knew Jennifer seems to be the right place to ask those questions. Teens always talk to other teens. I'm just trying to help out."

This seemed to satisfy him, and his shoulders relaxed. "Couldn't leave the detective work in Boston, huh?"

"Something like that."

"Well, I wish I could help, but, wait...hold on," he said, and called out to a couple standing a few yards away, motioning them over.

"Hey, Bailey," the man said, shaking Bailey's hand.

"Dani, you remember Toby White?" Bailey asked, gesturing toward the man. "And this is his wife, Tina. Toby, you knew Jennifer Cartwright pretty well, right?"

"Some, I guess."

"Did you ever hear about her having a boyfriend at the time she died or...."

Bailey repeated the same questions Dani had posed, eventually handing Toby and his wife off to her. As others approached just to make general conversation, Dani made the same inquiries after quick reintroductions, hugs and handshakes.

Adrenaline coursed through her as she peppered classmate after classmate with the same questions, hoping that eventually she might find someone who remembered something, no matter how trivial, that could help. With thoughts of Bailey King and his singledom long forgotten, she went from the bar to the dance floor to tables, chatting and questioning as she went. Forty-five minutes later, as she stood beside the punch table finishing up with three not-so-helpful couples, Peter and Amy approached, laughing as they came off the dance floor.

"I am getting too pregnant for this," Amy joked, reaching for a cup of non-alcoholic punch.

"Don't be ridiculous," Peter said, grabbing a beer from the bartender. "You're keeping up with the best of them." He sidled up to Dani. "Hey there, kiddo," he said, bumping shoulders with her. "You've got quite the audience going here."

"She's *investigating*," replied a woman in a tight-fitting red sheath dress, standing across from Dani in the little circle.

"Oh, yeah? Investigating what?" Despite the question, his frown told Dani he knew *exactly* what.

"Jennifer Cartwright's murder," said the woman, whose name tag read, "Denise Foley, Class of 1998."

Peter's expression grew more dour. "Oh, really?"

"I'm not investigating," Dani said. "I'm just asking a few questions about...well, the boyfriend Jennifer had that summer and another person—someone giving her a hard time—that she was concerned about." Peter already knew all this, but she said it for the sake of the group. She tried to keep her tone light, but his jaw had seized and his face was stony.

"I thought you were done with that," he snapped.

"Well—"

"Seriously, Dani—when?" His voice was raised now, with a sharp, frustrated edge to it. "When are you going to be done with this?" Amy moved in behind him, her face wrinkling in consternation.

"Well, I don't know, Peter," said Dani, and she could hear frustration bleeding into her tone as well. "I guess when I feel I've done everything I can to clear Dr. Beecher."

"Clear him?" He was nearly yelling now, apparently audible even over the music booming through the speakers, given that heads several yards away were turning in their direction. "Clear him? He *killed* her Dani. Killed her!"

Amy placed a hand on Peter's arm. "Peter—"

He shook his wife's hand off, but did lower his voice as the others in the circle, looking quite uncomfortable now, made subtle steps to back away. "No. Amy, look, Dani is one of my oldest and dearest friends and I'm so tired of watching this eat away at her year after year. Jennifer's *dead*. Dr. Beecher's *dead*. There's nothing more to do. There's no one to save! Whoever this boyfriend and the creep are, it doesn't matter because the case was solved years ago and Dr. Beecher got what he deserved." Throwing his hands up in surrender, he backed away. "I need some air," he said, and strode out of the room.

"It's not you," Amy offered kindly, her short, cocoa-brown hair swishing as she turned to Dani. "He's always been sensitive about the Jennifer Cartwright thing and how it affects you. He knows what it did to you back then and hates to see it still affecting you now."

Peter may have just yelled at her and walked out in anger, but even so, embers of adoration flickered in Dani's heart. While Sasha had been her partner in crime through the years, Peter had been her rock. Especially when it came to Jennifer Cartwright and dealing with the trauma in the aftermath. Sasha had been her encourager, her cheerleader, dragging her out to parties and school events and refusing to let her wallow; Peter had been her sympathizer, sitting with her more nights than she could count, his arm around her, quietly providing support. Literally letting her cry on his shoulder. Even crying with her too...

*Creep.*

The word, unbidden, resonated in her mind, and a bomb-shell exploded within her.

*Creep!*

"Dani? What is it?" Amy asked, her eyes growing large at whatever dumbstruck expression had overtaken Dani's face.

But Dani couldn't answer. She couldn't think. Her heart was thundering in her ears. Racing away. *Pounding, pounding...*

"Dani," Amy said, shaking her. "Are you okay?"

"I, um, I just...with Dr. Beecher today, and my parents, and now this...I just need a minute. I'm going to the restroom for a sec, okay?'

"Sure, yeah," Amy said, her voice ripe with worry. "Do you need me to go with—"

"No, thanks," Dani cut her off, already moving toward the exit.

*Pounding, pounding, pounding...her heart slamming against her ribs.* She pushed through the lightheadedness threatening to overtake her, forcing herself to walk calmly, until she reached the door at the back of the room and slipped through.

The second it shut behind her she began running.

She crashed through the door leading out of the front of the building into the still, muggy air, frantically scanning the parking lot. After two passes she saw Peter, standing alone in the dark at the far left corner of the building, staring up at the sky. She hurtled to him, grabbing onto both arms, twisting him toward her as his face snapped down to meet hers.

"It's you, isn't it?" she asked.

He wrenched out of her grip. His gaze, normally so warm and inviting, was like granite. "I don't know what you're talking about."

Dani's heart imploded. *Oh, Peter.* "The boyfriend. Jennifer's boyfriend. It was you."

His frame collapsed on itself and he seemed to shrink, as if her words had knocked down the very supports that had been holding him up all these years—the bars of the cage in which he had locked up this secret for so long. "How...how did you know?"

A solitary tear rolled down her face. She hadn't wanted to be right. "*Creep.* You called the stalker a 'creep.' Jennifer called him that in her diary, but you haven't seen the diary. At least not since I found it. And I never mentioned the term 'creep' to any of you. The only person Jennifer used that word with was her boyfriend."

Peter's hands went to his hips, his head dropping even lower. Dani moved to embrace him and he jerked back out of her reach as if he were tainted. As if he were afraid for her to touch him.

She stood her ground. "Why didn't you say something, Peter?"

"When—now or then?" he asked, his voice trembling.

"Either?" she answered gently.

"It's a long story."

# 18

"We started dating at the end of our sophomore year." Dani and Peter sat on a bench outside the Civic Center, in an area off to the side that held several picnic tables. His body was rigid, facing forward, while she curved toward him. She had to fight every instinct she had to not pull him close, hug him tightly and swear that everything would be okay. The pain he was feeling was nearly tangible, engraved in every wrinkle in his tortured expression.

"She and I were a strange match. She was the popular kid, I was the artistic oddball. It was like some kind of lame teen movie premise." He let a sad chuckle escape, but his visage remained dark.

"Why didn't you tell us?"

"Because I was afraid. Afraid of what you'd say. Afraid it wouldn't last—that she'd grow tired of me and dump me and then I'd look like an idiot. And Chip Matthews had a crush on her—I didn't want him and his football buddies shoving me in a locker or something. It was just easier to keep it to ourselves."

"Which is what she wanted too."

"Sort of. She didn't want her parents to know, so she was happy with us not telling anyone, because it would get back to them. She thought they would have a problem with me—unpopular kid, not the best grades, and worst of all, absolutely no money. Her family lived in Deerfield Meadows and owned half the rental real estate in the county. We lived in a trailer park and my dad mowed yards for a living."

"There's nothing wrong with that."

"No, but she was sure they wouldn't like it. And she made me swear to not even tell my own parents. Eventually, though, I didn't care. I didn't care who knew at school and I actually wanted her parents to know. I felt like I was living a lie. I didn't like hiding things from them. I felt she was ashamed of me. Eventually, we started fighting about it—well, you probably know that, don't you? You read her diary."

"But when she was killed—why didn't you say something then?"

"Because I was terrified they would think I did it. I knew about that diary. She always had it with her. She didn't trust leaving it anywhere. Not even at home. Didn't want her parents to find it. She wrote *everything* in there. Called it her "silent best friend." She promised that she hadn't mentioned me by name, but I didn't know what else was in there. I figured that eventually they would find the diary and realize there was a boyfriend, and they'd start looking at him as a suspect. I was fifteen, Dani. *Fifteen*. I was scared that if they knew I was the boyfriend, they'd think I did it. It didn't help that the ring I gave her—the one with the twisted vines—was taken. I thought that only made me look more guilty."

"What about after the diary wasn't found?"

"It didn't change anything. What if I came forward as the boyfriend no one knew about? They might still pin it on me."

"But the stalker...this creep she talked about...you knew

about him. You could have told the police. They would've had a lead."

Peter shook his head. "She never told me who it was. And from what you've told us about the diary, she didn't identify him in there either. But I did think about it, Dani. I did." He sniffed, glancing away from her, staring into the dark. "About a week afterward, when the diary still hadn't been mentioned and they hadn't come looking for me, I thought about saying something."

"Why didn't you?'

"Because they arrested Dr. Beecher. They found her bracelet in his house and I just knew he had done it. And then later, with what his daughter said about them arguing and him following after her when she headed for the river...and then the DNA evidence, his skin under her nails...there was no doubt in my mind that he was guilty and that there wasn't a point in coming forward. I even thought that maybe Dr. Beecher was the creep she was talking about..."

"No. She mentioned the creep before she started working for Dr. Beecher. She was excited about that job. She wouldn't have taken it or written about it like that if Dr. Beecher was the creep."

"But the DNA evidence, the footprints—"

"That evidence only proves they had contact and you know as well as I do that Dr. Beecher explained it. His daughter misinterpreted things. They weren't arguing. Jennifer was upset about something that day—probably the ongoing disagreement between the two of you—and was crying when Dr. Beecher came home. She wouldn't talk about what it was and ran out. He followed her down to the river and she slipped. He grabbed her to stop her from falling and she scratched him in the process. She begged him to just leave her alone, and he did. He went back in the house and when he eventually saw that her bike wasn't there, he thought she'd gone home."

Peter remained silent, his face grim.

"He didn't do it, Peter."

"Well, I didn't do it." Then suddenly his eyes flashed to hers, something desperate in them. "Wait, you don't think I'd...Dani, I would never—"

She grabbed his hand, squeezing it. "Of course not! No, I know you couldn't." And she meant it. The boyfriend hadn't done it, because the boyfriend was her best friend and it just wasn't possible.

"I loved her, Dani. I really did. It broke me when she died, and I couldn't tell a soul." A shadow of shame lay beneath the rivulets of tears cascading down his cheeks. "I should have been there that afternoon. I was supposed to be there. We were going to meet at the shed after she got off work and try to figure it all out. But Dad insisted that I stay at the house and help him work on the car. It was a two-man job. I couldn't meet her and I had no way to let her know." He sniffed again. "All this time I've thought, what if I'd been there? What if I could have stopped it? Maybe she'd still be alive."

"You don't know that. And you might have been killed too. It's not your fault."

He rubbed his eyes, then flicked his gaze to her. "Part of me was actually glad you were so distraught after finding her, that it tore you up so much, because that meant I had an excuse to be sad, because I could be sad with you, cry with you, be depressed with you and it would look like I was just hurting for my friend, not like I was devastated because of her, which I could have never explained." He shook his head. "I was a terrible person."

"You weren't. You were a scared, broken-hearted kid."

"That's what I've been telling myself for thirteen years. But then you found her diary...and it just brought it all back. I was so thrilled when you said that she didn't mention me by name."

She nodded, imagining the terror he must have felt at that

first dinner at Sasha's when she told them what she had found in the shed.

"Dani...I've never wavered from my belief that Dr. Beecher was guilty—I had to cling to that to stay sane, to know that I didn't somehow derail the investigation by not speaking up. Then today...I can't get past the timing, Dani. You give him a copy of the diary and he gets killed the next day. And suddenly I'm really wondering if someone...if that stalker—"

"If someone else was responsible."

With the tiniest of motions, he bobbed his head. "But I'm still not any help, Dani. Jennifer didn't tell me who he was."

"What about the girl she was trying to protect? The one Jennifer initially saw with the creep? Jennifer wrote that she confronted her about it, but never identified who the girl was."

"She wouldn't tell me who the girl was either. I asked, but she was adamant about keeping it private. Jennifer was a vault. There was no end to the secrets she knew."

"You'd think she would have at least told someone. Maybe her best friend? Kendall?" Dani suggested.

"The police questioned Kendall back when it happened, didn't they? If she had known something, she would have told them." Even as he said it, Dani remembered the short page of notes in the police file from their interview of Kendall. There had been no mention of a stalker.

"I haven't seen her tonight," Dani said. "I looked for her earlier, but—"

"I saw her come in about fifteen minutes ago. I heard her say her flight was late."

If Kendall was there, maybe all wasn't lost. Maybe Dani could still get some answers. Her nerves tingling at the prospect, she stood, squeezing his shoulder. "I'm so sorry that you've had to carry this by yourself all these years, Peter. I wish you would have told me."

"It's my own fault. But just keep me out of it if you can. Amy doesn't know and I should probably tell her myself. If I need to come clean about it with the police, I will, but—"

"Let's just see how this goes, okay?"

He nodded, and offered a faint smile. Leaving him there, she walked back to the entrance, sparing one last look at him as she grabbed the door handle. He was still sitting, his hands folded in his lap, staring into the night sky and likely wondering, she thought, about the million other ways this might have turned out if he had only said something before now.

# 19

When Dani spotted Kendall St. James at a table across the room, she was raising a glass in a toast Dani couldn't hear with several others gathered around her. Zeroing in on the petite woman, Dani made a beeline through the throngs, ignoring several greetings as she shot through the space. Kendall was taking a drink in honor of the toast when Dani arrived at her arm.

"Dani Lake!" Kendall screamed, leaning in for an exaggerated hug, and Dani felt what she presumed to be splashes of martini dripping down her bare arm.

"Hi, Kendall. It's good to see you."

"And you! And everybody," Kendall raved, waving a hand around the room. Back in the day, Kendall had been the most exuberant cheerleader on the Warriors' squad, and it seemed she hadn't lost a bit of that enthusiasm. "I hate I was late. Our plane was delayed out of Dallas—"

"Kendall, could I speak to you for a minute? Privately?" Dani asked, tugging gently on Kendall's arm.

"Well, sure. I'll be right back, y'all," Kendall said, setting her glass down and grinning widely, her snow-white teeth reflecting the pink hues of the DJ's lights.

They stepped several yards away to an unoccupied spot against the wall. "Kendall, I want to ask you some questions about Jennifer."

Kendall's grin evaporated. "Jennifer? Cartwright? Why? I know I missed her tribute, but I'm sure—"

"No, it's not that. Her diary's been...found recently and it mentions something about a person who might have had a grudge against her around the time she died."

"What?" Kendall asked, genuine surprise flashing in her features.

"She wrote that she knew a secret about someone—a male— and that when she confronted him about it, he didn't take it well. He may have even started stalking her. Does that ring a bell at all?"

Kendall shook her head. "I never knew anything about a stalker." Her lips pursed. "No, Jen would have told me if she had a stalker. What exactly was she supposed to have confronted this person about?"

"Apparently Jennifer witnessed something, something between another girl and this male that was inappropriate or wrong somehow. She says she eventually confronted the girl first, but the girl denied everything. Then Jennifer started noticing that the male was acting differently around her, like he knew she knew something. One day she happened to see him carrying on the same way with another girl—she never said exactly what was going on, but it was clear it wasn't right. So she confronted him, threatening to tell—" Dani cut herself off, noticing that Kendall's face had lost all color.

"She confronted him?" Kendall's tone was flat, and her gaze seemed to drift off, unfocused.

"Kendall?"

Kendall's gaze returned to Dani. "Jen never told me any of

that. She never said—" Kendall sucked in a quivering breath. "Where's her diary? Where is it?"

"The police have it." Dani didn't feel the need to share that there was another copy at the prison and one on her kitchen table.

"So, why are *you* asking questions?" Kendall asked, a tremor in her voice.

"I'm the one who found it. And though the police have been...reviewing it, I'm also a police detective in Boston and I happened to be here, and well, this case has always been close to my heart."

"Because you're the one who found Jen." Kendall's tone was softer, laced with quiet respect.

Dani nodded. "And because I've never believed that Dr. Beecher was actually guilty. Kendall, with this diary, there's finally evidence to suggest that someone else may have killed Jennifer. So, if you know something, if you can shed any light on this man she confronted or the girl—"

"It was me." The admission was a whisper, barely audible over the din.

"You?"

Kendall nodded.

"But then...why wouldn't you have told the police about him when they questioned you?"

"Told them what? I had no idea that he had any connection to Jen! All she said when she came to me was that she had a gut feeling something was going on between me and him that shouldn't be. I denied it and we never said another word about it. She never told me that she'd actually seen anything." Her hands flew to her mouth, cupping it, her face twisted in horror. "But she must've, right? If she was willing to confront him? Oh, how could I have been so stupid?" The words were coming in torrents now. "I thought she forgot about it. And I was so freaked out that she had noticed, I immediately ended things with him." She dropped her head into her hands, covering her face as she shook it back and forth. "I thought that was the end of it! I *tried* to forget about it. I tried really hard." She ripped her hands from her face, her mascara now streaked over her cheekbones. "But now you're telling me he got involved with another girl? What if there were others? I was so young, I didn't think about the next person—"

"What happened, Kendall?" Dani's heart raced. She was so close. "Who was it?"

Kendall ignored the questions, steamrolling Dani, continuing to spew her tortured diatribe. "If Jen had *told* me any of that, if she had told me what she saw and what she did...I would have known to say something to the police." She lashed out, desperately clutching Dani's arm, her eyes wild. "What if it wasn't Dr. Beecher at all? What if *he* killed her because she was going to tell, and got away with it—"

"Kendall," Dani said firmly, grasping the woman's upper arms to hold her still. "Slow down. Breathe."

Kendall grew quiet, her trembling body in Dani's grip, her shoulders rising and falling in time with her spastic, exaggerated breaths.

"Okay," Dani said. "Now tell me—who is *he?*"

Kendall whimpered, then uttered a name.

# 20

Dani's mind churned as her car sped through the streets of Skye toward home. She had barely managed a rushed, "I've gotta go," to Sasha before dashing out of the reunion, ignoring her friend's shouts of, "Where are you going?" sounding behind her.

The streets were desolate at this hour, her car zooming along unhindered. She forced herself to breathe with intentional rhythm—four in, four hold, four out—trying to rein in the adrenaline that was making it difficult to process, to plan.

*What now? It's Saturday night! What can I get—*

Spotting the red light at the last instant, she jammed her foot on the brake, the car violently jerking to a stop just past the lane line. She pounded her fists on the wheel, willing the light to turn.

She could call the Chief and explain what she had just learned from Kendall. That *had* to be enough to justify another look at the situation. *Right?* But would he listen? He would have to, with this kind of allegation. Even if it turned out to be of no help in Jennifer's case. But it was just Kendall's word and after so long—

The light turned green and she gunned it.

*Chris.*

If she could get him to back her up, maybe together they could convince the Chief.

Violating her own rules about calling while driving, she blindly dug her cell from her purse and dialed Chris, now exceedingly grateful that he had insisted she take his number. It went to voicemail.

"Chris, hi...listen, I'm sorry to call you like this, so late, but I need your help. You said that if you could help, you would, and I think I've just stumbled onto something really big. But I need your support to take it to the Chief. I'm headed home, but will you call me as soon as you get this? Or just come over, okay? Thanks, bye."

She hung up and pressed harder on the gas.

DANI BARRELED into the kitchen from the garage, heading straight for her bedroom.

*Get out of this dress. Get the diary, get the file—*

She had just made it to the hallway when suddenly someone grabbed her from behind, strong arms clenching around her middle. She screamed and a hand shot upward, clapping over her mouth, muffling the sound. Cold panic coursed through her like lightning, but only for a few seconds. Then her training kicked in and panic turned to controlled ferocity. Because both arms were pinned beneath the attacker's hold, she twisted her shoulders back and forth violently, in the process catching a flash of the ski mask covering his head and what might have been a black jacket. His grip loosened just enough so that she could move her right arm, which instinctively flew to her hip, something she immediately realized was pointless. Her pistol was lying beneath her pillow. There had been no way to wear it with that dress.

She reached up and yanked hard on the arm covering her mouth, but the hand didn't budge. Electricity crackled across her skin as he gripped her tighter, and she began kicking as he dragged her backward into the living room. She tried to get a foothold, tried to get some leverage so she could land a good kick, but he moved her too fast and too hard and smashed her against a wall, forcing her face into it as he twisted her one free arm behind her back and pulled up, wrenching it hard.

"Ahhh!" she cried angrily, the severe pain in her shoulder momentarily disabling her. He slammed himself against her, trapping her whole body against the wall.

"You. Are. Done. You hear me?" he growled, his breath hot on her neck. His words were low and guttural, but unnaturally so, as if intentionally modified. She said nothing and continued struggling.

He stepped back, pulling her with him, then slammed her against the wall again. "Are you finished?"

Dani's pulse thundered in her head. His grip was like a vise. She nodded, relenting.

"Good. This is over. It stops now. No more digging. Unless you want to end up like Beecher. Got it?" The hand on her face tightened, squeezing her cheeks against her skull. "Do you understand? Nod once if you understand."

She nodded.

"I'm leaving. Do not turn around. I mean it. I'm armed. I don't want to shoot you, but I will."

And then, he let go. Quick, shuffling steps sounded behind her. She gave it three seconds before turning.

He was gone.

She ran to her bedroom, snatched her pistol from beneath her pillow and raced after him, flying through the kitchen door into the garage, then out onto the driveway. She skidded to a stop, swiveling left and right, scanning for any sign of movement, the darkness broken only by the streetlamp at the bottom of the driveway.

*Nothing.*

For several minutes Dani strained, listening for footsteps, a rustling in the grass, anything that might reveal him. But all was quiet—just crickets and a soft breeze that kicked her hair up around her face.

*My phone.*

But it was inside.

*I should call...who? 9-1-1? The Chief? Yeah, the Chief...*

She started jogging back toward the garage, and had just reached the door when headlights flashed behind her and she turned. A truck was coming up her driveway. It stopped just feet from her. Chris jumped out.

"I got your message and I—" He stopped talking mid-stride, concern flooding his features as he closed the distance between them, his gaze drifting to her weapon, then back up. "Someone was here again, weren't they?" He grabbed her arm. "Are you okay? What happened?"

"He was inside when I got home," she said evenly. Now that the immediate danger had passed, her breathing was returning to normal, her pulse steadying. "He attacked me, then ran out. He's gone."

Chris's expression hardened, as he cast around, searching. "You're sure? He's not still here?" he asked, before leveling his gaze at her again.

She nodded. "He's gone. Come on inside. I've got a lot to tell you."

# 21

"I don't like it," Chris said, dropping onto the couch as Dani moved to sit across from him in her father's chair. "You need to call this in." The entire way inside the house he had hounded her to report the attack.

"No," she insisted for the third time, a little frustrated that he wouldn't drop it, and anxious to get to the reason she had called him in the first place. "He's not coming back tonight. I was going to call it in, but now that you're here there's no point in dragging anyone else out. I'll file a report in the morning, I promise, but look—don't you see?" Dani could hear the excitement in her voice as she rushed on. "This means something, the fact that this happened. *I was right.* There's more to this case. They'll have to open it back up. That's why I called you—"

"I tried to call you back as soon as I got the message, but you didn't answer, so—"

"Chris," she interrupted, leaning toward him, "I found out who Jennifer's stalker was."

Chris's mouth dropped slightly, forming a compressed "O." "That's the something big you stumbled onto?"

She nodded. "It came out at the reunion. The girl Jennifer mentions in the diary, the one that she confronted about the man she calls "the creep"—that girl was her best friend Kendall."

"How did you figure that out?"

"I was randomly asking people about what Jennifer had written, if the things she said meant anything to them. I...um, eventually ended up talking to Kendall," she said, purposely skipping the part where she realized that Peter was the boyfriend, and that he had directed her to Kendall. She proceeded to recount her entire conversation with Kendall for him, including the woman's shock over learning Jennifer had confronted the man Jennifer had called the "creep."

"...and that's when she just broke. Confessed that *she* was the girl Jennifer had originally confronted about him."

"So, who was he?" Chris asked.

"Lyle Rheardon. Our sophomore English teacher. He was new then, just out of college, only six or seven years older than we were. She didn't mention him when the police questioned her in connection with Jennifer's murder, because she didn't know about Jennifer confronting him, and had no reason to believe Rheardon had a problem with Jennifer or a reason to hurt her. She didn't connect the two at all."

A grim look stole over Chris's face. "Rheardon's the high school principal now, since last year."

"I know. Kendall told me."

"So, Rheardon was having a relationship with a student—"

"*Students*, according to what Jennifer wrote in her diary about the other girl at the theater. It's what made her finally threaten to expose him."

"That's a pretty good motive for murder."

"That's what I'm saying! It's a reason, Chris. A *real* reason for the D.A. to look at someone other than Dr. Beecher." A band tightened around Dani's chest, her throat suddenly raw. "Even if it won't help him now, it could clear his name. It could change everything for his children."

Chris leaned back, biting his lip before he spoke. "Is Kendall willing to talk to the police?"

"She is. She's completely sick about it, thinking that if she'd said something back when Rheardon was involved with her, she could've stopped him from seeking out other girls. Could've maybe even stopped Jennifer's murder."

"Kendall was what, fifteen, sixteen then? She can't carry that blame."

He was right and a pang of sympathy for Kendall reverberated through Dani. She knew all too well what it was like to carry guilt from a young age. She had carried so much of it herself after finding Jennifer, for being the person who had in effect set in motion the events which ultimately led to Dr. Beecher's conviction, and then being completely powerless to do anything to help him, something she had spent the rest of her life yearning to do. "Self-blame is hard to shake. Even when you know it really wasn't your fault."

"You realize, that with this kind of allegation, no matter what they may think about a possible connection to Jennifer's murder, they're going to want to talk to Rheardon. It's a separate issue," Chris said. "These are felonies we're talking about. Even if they can't connect him to the murder they'll consider prosecuting him for those alone—if there's anything to prosecute."

"What's the statute of limitations on something like that here?"

"Depends on what happened exactly. But if he did have a relationship with any of those minors, he'll be in real trouble." Chris's eyes narrowed. "Could it have been Rheardon who attacked you tonight?"

"I don't know. I haven't seen him in years."

Chris pulled out his cell phone, tapped on it and waited as a photo slowly materialized. He held the screen out to her. "Was it him?"

The man in the photo on the Skye High School website was in his mid-thirties, sandy-haired with a narrow face and cheerful eyes. He was nice-looking, though not strikingly so. The head shot was only from the chest up, but it looked like he was hefty, maybe a weightlifter, with a bit of a wrestler's build. She had only seen flashes of her attacker in the struggle, and he had been wearing a ski mask, but it was possible. "Maybe," she finally said. "His face was covered and it all happened so fast. I didn't get a good look. It's hard to tell from the photo, but I can't rule it out. This guy was strong and Rheardon looks like he would be. Maybe if I heard Rheardon's voice? But, I'm pretty sure the guy was doing his best to disguise it, so I don't know if that will help."

"I don't want you staying here alone. Whoever it was might come back. Come with me. I can take you to Sasha's place if you want. You'll be safer there."

While she appreciated the concern and the undercurrent of chivalry, she had no intention of leaving. She was perfectly capable of protecting herself, the events of earlier notwithstanding.

"Thanks, but I'm not being chased out of my own home. He surprised me once, but not again." She pointed to her pistol on the coffee table. "I'm armed. I can handle it. What I want to know is, where do we go from here?"

Chris eyed her silently, possibly considering whether to fight her on the issue. His posture was rigid, as if her insistence on staying was bordering on annoying him—like she was a petulant child refusing to do what was best. But eventually, after narrowing his eyes skeptically and exhaling in disgruntled surrender, he moved on. "I'll talk to the Chief. Get the ball rolling. We'll reach out to Kendall and, ultimately, talk to Rheardon if there's enough to go on." He stood. "I'll keep you posted as much as I can."

She rose too. "Thanks. I mean it. You're the only one who's supported me on this. It means a lot."

He smiled, reached out, and squeezed her arm. "Look, if you still have a copy of the diary, it might help for me to take it back to the Chief since the D.A. has the original. And it wouldn't hurt if I got the file back from you too," he said, his eyebrows raised.

"Yeah, of course. They're just in here," she replied, waving for him to follow her into the kitchen.

She halted abruptly in the doorway, an icy knife cutting through her. The diary and the file, both of which she had left on the table before heading to the reunion, were gone.

"What is it?" Chris said, coming up behind her, peering over her shoulder.

She extended a hand outward, pointing. "They were right there on the table. He must've taken them."

Chris pushed by her and circled the table, as if double-checking, then stood still, putting his hands on his hips. "It's fine. It'll be fine. The file from the Chief was just a copy, right? And the diary we can request from the D.A.'s office. I doubt they've turned it over to Jennifer's parents already."

*He's right. The Chief has the original file and the D.A. has the original diary. And there's even another copy of the diary at the prison.*

*Which means this makes absolutely no sense.*

"I don't understand," she said. "If other copies exist, why would he bother taking these?"

Chris didn't have an answer.

Five minutes later, after trying and failing once more to convince Dani to go with him, he had driven away and Dani had locked herself inside the house. She snuggled into her father's chair, a fleece blanket tucked in tightly around her, her cold pistol resting in her lap waiting beneath her ready hand.

# 22

Dani yawned quietly, quickly throwing up a hand to hide it from the others in the row of chairs. She wasn't fast enough, though, and Sasha, sitting on her left, her four-year-old between them, shot her an amused look. Dani wrinkled her nose abashedly, and Sasha let out a soft, good-natured snort, before turning forward again.

*What am I doing here?*

Dani honestly couldn't remember how Sasha had twisted her arm into coming to services that morning. It had sort of vaguely been in the plans from the beginning—tag along with Sasha's family to church followed by a full lunch at Sasha's that afternoon. But after a long, sleep-deprived night in her father's chair—she'd only gotten a couple of hours at most—she had decided to cancel. Sasha had, of course, beaten her to it, calling at eight o'clock with one of the kids bawling in the background, to remind her that they would be swinging by to get her at nine. She refused to hear any grumblings about not coming, and also demanded Dani provide a full explanation of her rushed exit from the reunion once they had a chance to talk. Too tired to argue, Dani had pulled on a pair of dark casual pants and a cream top with lace trim and met them with a travel mug of extra-strong coffee when Sasha's minivan had pulled into the driveway.

Dani glanced to her left to take in the little family: Trent, then Sasha with her arm around him, and beside her, Willett, holding their wriggling daughter, Alana. It was the perfect family portrait. Something she had hoped to have with Finn, but never would. Even if they had stayed together, she doubted they would have ever sat in services like this. Finn had never had much to do with religion. And though she had grown up going to church—just down the street from here, in fact—after finding Jennifer she had simply lost all interest. Her parents continued going, but she fought them every Sunday, dragging her feet and bellyaching, until finally they just gave up.

A sudden increase in the pastor's volume snagged Dani's wandering attention. The energetic forty-something with auburn hair was tall and imposing, but with a kind, welcoming face, and at the moment was talking about building a house on a rock.

"...This world is unstable. This world is ever-changing." His enthusiastic words reverberated through the sanctuary, a wide room divided by two aisles into three sections, each with two dozen rows of chairs. The place was packed, but the microphone affixed to the acrylic podium carried his voice to every ear. "The only thing you can count on in this world is that you cannot count on the things of this world. But the wise man builds his house upon the Rock. Because the Rock is stable. Unchanging. And though the world falls away, the Rock remains."

His words pricked a memory from her youth. A song about a wise man and a flood. A tune rattled around Dani's brain.

*The wise man built his house upon the rock.*
*The wise man built his house upon the rock.*

*The rains came down and the floods came up.*
*But the house on the rock stood firm.*

She had not thought of those words in years.

It wasn't that she didn't believe. It was just that after finding Jennifer Cartwright, God simply hadn't made sense any more. She couldn't reconcile it. Because the only thing that had made sense was that someone should be able to make it right—at least make sure that Jennifer's killer was brought to justice. But that hadn't happened. No one had made it right and instead, an innocent man had gone to jail.

That reality had forever altered the course of Dani's life, because the tragedy had consumed her. This need to have the murder solved, to have the person responsible pay and Dr. Beecher cleared—*that* need had become her obsession, a burning ember deep within her that had never gone out and, if she was honest, had fueled her ever since. It had, in so many ways, been the foundation she had built her life, her identity, on.

She had become a police officer because of that murder, because of a need to never, ever, let something like that happen again. Not that she regretted her choice. She loved being a police detective. But, if she was honest, sometimes she did wonder what she might have become if she had never ventured over to the honeysuckle that day. Before that day, she and Dr. Beecher had often spoken of her becoming a doctor. If she had never found Jennifer, is that the path she would have taken? How else would her life be different?

These weren't new notions. More than once her counseling sessions with Dr. Joline had exposed the fact that Jennifer's murder was the driving force behind her decisions and focus, the proverbial dog forever nipping at her heels. But sitting here now, on the brink of possibly solving the case that had been her reason for everything, a curious thought occurred to her.

*If it is solved—what then?*

If this latest lead panned out, if Rheardon proved to be the killer, what did that mean for her?

*I would be thrilled. No question.*

*But what about the aftermath?* What would happen if the subtext of her entire adult life simply was no more? She closed her eyes and tried to imagine it.

*No more wound, deep and dark, always raw and seeping, never healing. No more unanswered questions. No more guilt over being the one who started it all, then left it unfinished.*

Case solved. Burden lifted.

*Free.*

But there was...something else too. Lurking behind the promise of freedom was another, less welcome outcome. Startled, Dani's eyes flicked open.

Emptiness. Absence. A hollowed out place where purpose ought to be.

She realized she was holding her breath and expelled a quiet hiss of air, letting her shoulders drop.

It wasn't unheard of—detectives chasing a difficult case for years and years, then finally solving it, only to discover that its resolution left a black hole behind. These were dangerous things, these black holes, especially if one chose to fill it with alcohol or overwork or other destructive vices. Shifting in her seat, Dani tightened the muscles in her stomach.

*This is crazy. You're being crazy. There are other murders to solve. Other people to save. If you solve this one, you'll just move on to the next.*

Because there would always be another.

## 23

Dani and Sasha stood over the sink in Sasha's kitchen, Sasha washing and Dani drying the larger items and non-dishwasher-safe utensils. The boys and Amy had prepared lunch and now were playing outside with the kids while Sasha and Dani tidied up. The minute the others had gone out the door, Sasha had pressed Dani for details about her sudden departure from the reunion.

"All I can tell you is that there's been a break in the case," Dani said, drying a glass baking dish, now empty of the lasagna that had been devoured at lunch. "I can't say any more. But I really think this might be it."

"Did you call Chris about it?"

Dani cut her eyes at Sasha. A tiny grin curved the corner of Sasha's mouth. "Why would you ask that?"

Sasha shrugged. "Just a hunch."

"Welllll..." Dani said, drawing the word out, "yes, I did."

"I knew it!"

Dani put up a hand to stop the mental train Sasha was about to jump on. "But only because he's a detective and the only one who's offered to help me in this," Dani quickly defended, deciding to leave out any of the more...interesting details.

She could only imagine what Sasha would think if she knew how Chris had wanted to come to her rescue last night, insisting that he deliver her to Sasha's after the attack. But Dani hadn't told Sasha or the others about being assaulted in the house. She didn't see the point in worrying them, and they never would have let it go. She would go in and make a report about it first thing Monday morning, although it was likely Chris had already told the Chief by now.

She hadn't heard from Chris since last night, which wasn't really a surprise. If he was working the case, he would have had his hands full all day. Still, she was a little disappointed to not have gotten even the tiniest update.

*Surely by morning he'll get in touch with news about their progress—progress toward finally solving Jennifer's murder.*

This thought returned Dani to her earlier ruminations about life after Jennifer Cartwright.

"Sash, I've been thinking," Dani said, as Sasha handed her a dripping wet cookie sheet that had been used to bake garlic bread. She ran the soft yellow-and-white-striped cotton towel over the metal sheet. "What happens—as in, what does it mean for me—if this works out and Jennifer's case is finally solved?"

Sasha turned toward her, her eyebrows drawn together. "What do you mean?"

After a moment's hesitation, Dani rehashed for Sasha the mental hoops she had been jumping through during the service. She pivoted, facing away from the sink, then leaned against it. "My whole life has been built on this murder. On this injustice. At some point, I don't know, I think it became a part of me. A part of the fabric of who I am—worrying about it, yearning for it to be solved, defining my years here and my years after, my choices. I'm not sure who I am without it there in the background, fueling the purpose driving me. If it's solved —*when* it's solved—that purpose disappears."

"It doesn't disappear. It's fulfilled. You've worked hard to have it solved properly and if it is, then you've succeeded."

"I know, but...what if everything I've built wasn't really about me, but was about this...this *thing* in my past? And if that's true, what happens when it's gone? What if the life I have isn't really the life I wanted or needed? What if it's just the one I created as a reaction to what happened to me thirteen years ago?"

Sasha looked down at the suds in the sink. Dani breathed in their clean, lemon scent that energized the air as she waited for her friend to answer. After a few seconds, Sasha looked up, stared out the window over the sink at her family playing in the yard, and smiled.

"Did I ever tell you what my mother said to me right after Trent was born?" she asked, her eyes not straying from the scene outside.

"No, not that I remember."

"She sat right down in my hospital room, with me holding that brand-new baby in my arms and said, 'Sasha, I need you to remember something. You are gonna love this baby more than life itself. Your whole world is gonna change because of this baby and it can be real easy to lose sight of yourself when that happens. Because children are wonderful, but they are hard. There are joys and disappointments, mountains and valleys. And hardest of all, someday—someday this child will leave. And so it's important, it's crucial for you to remember that while this act of being a momma is your mission—and it's *the* most important mission you can have, and you should be a momma of excellence—it's not your identity. It's what you're doing. It's not who you are.'"

"What's the difference?" Dani asked.

"That's what I said."

"And?"

"She said, 'If you allow this child alone to define you, then when parenting gets hard or you think you've failed, or when he grows up and leaves—you will be left struggling and confused and wondering what the point of you is. So define yourself by something greater. Something unchanging. *Someone* unchanging.'" Sasha's gaze drifted from the window to Dani, her eyes full of warmth.

"Build it upon a rock?" Dani offered discerningly.

Sasha's lips puckered in a tight smile. "You were listening today."

"And you think that's all it takes."

"I think that you aren't Jennifer's case or any case you handle. Sure, what happened shaped you, but it isn't the whole of you. And when it's gone, you'll still be here. But I think you're smart to ask the question, because whether it's Jennifer's murder or the next one you handle in Boston, it's really easy to confuse what you do with who you are, and inevitably that will leave you unsatisfied and chasing after meaning. You don't think I worry about what my life will be like once my babies are gone? Once the job I've done for twenty-something years shifts into something completely different?"

"So what do you do? How do you deal with it?"

"I do what my momma told me. I trust that I am who God says I am—His child, who is well-loved, working out his plan for me—part of which is to be a momma of excellence to Alana and that crazy four-year-old boy out there," she said, pointing to Trent, spinning in wild circles on the grass. "Those truths do not and will not change. Ever. And I take great comfort in that."

"Hmm." Dani turned back around to the sink, picked up the towel and began drying a bowl. "You know, I didn't hate being there today."

"Maybe you should try out a service in Boston."

"Maybe I will."

Sasha dropped the last dirty pan in the sink and began scraping it with a scrubber, knocking shoulders with Dani. "I think Momma would say that's a really good idea. And," she paused dramatically, "you know who else wouldn't hate it?"

Dani stopped drying. "Who?"

"Bailey King. He was there today," Sasha said with a smirk, delivering the news as if it were a secret she'd sworn not to tell.

"Where? I didn't see him."

"You'd already gone outside with Trent. He came with his parents. Said he saw you from across the room, and that he talked to you last night, but you got away before he had a chance to spend any more time with you."

"We were catching up when...well, I got the information that opened up the case. I kind of just moved on through the crowd."

"Well, apparently he didn't move on. He was hinting around about getting your number."

"He was?"

Sasha nodded. "But I told him you were already spoken for by a certain police detective here in town."

Dani's face flushed with heat. "You didn't!"

Sasha laughed wickedly. "Of course I didn't." She grinned widely. "But I wanted to. I saw you and Chris out there on the porch the other night. You don't need some old fling stepping in to confuse things."

"Sasha, I'm serious. You have got to stop trying to set me up like this—"

"Are you really gonna stand there and tell me you don't like Chris?"

"No, I'm...yes, he's nice and he's been great and—"

"And he's handsome."

"Yeah, he's handsome—but look, this is ridiculous. I don't live here."

"Just a matter of geography, girl. I've seen the way that boy looks at you and you might think that he's a detective helping out on a murder case, but I'm telling you, that murder isn't the only thing he's working."

Dani rolled her eyes. "Just hand me the pan, already."

Sasha held it out to her, freshly rinsed and citrusy, when Dani's cell phone sounded. She pulled the phone from her pocket, her heart skipping a beat as she read the name "Chris Newton" on the caller ID.

## 24

The door to Chris Newton's condominium swung open, and he stood in the entryway, dressed in a black T-shirt and jeans, grinning ear to ear.

"You made it. Come on in."

"Of course, I made it! I'm dying to hear all about it," Dani said, brushing past him, immediately bathed in the heavenly scent of rosemary, roasting meat and something buttery. "Are you...cooking?" she asked, slightly confused as she walked farther inside. The space had an open floor plan, with the living room and its U-shaped leather couch separated from the kitchen by a huge island that contained the sink on one side and a high countertop on the other, with seating for four on wicker barstools. She stepped toward the bar, spotting gleaming pans on the stovetop and a light in the oven.

"Nothing gets past you, Detective," he said, winking.

"You really didn't—"

"Have a seat," he told her, nodding at the nearest barstool as he moved behind the island. "There's roasted almonds in the bowl there, if you're hungry, and that glass of ice water's for you." He pointed to a tumbler on her right. "Unless you want wine or something—"

"No, water's fine," she said, dropping her purse on the floor beside the stool and sliding onto the seat.

He slid a pan of rolls into the oven behind him, then turned to face her. "Well, I couldn't meet you until now, and *now* is dinnertime and I couldn't exactly take you out in public to talk about this, so I thought—dinner at home." He squinted, a hint of concern behind his eyes as he appraised her. "Should I not have? Was this a bad idea?"

The truth was, she was still full from lunch and was really too excited to even think about eating. But he had clearly gone to a lot of trouble, and what's more, done so after what must have been a jam-packed, exhausting day. "No, of course not, it's fine," she said, plastering on a grateful smile. "I'm just surprised, that's all. When you said you had news but you couldn't tell me over the phone I figured you'd just launch right into a rundown when I got here."

"No way. This is big! Huge. Deserves a proper celebration," he said, stepping to the oven again and bending over to examine its contents through the glass. "Another twenty minutes or so, I think," he said. "I hope you like Eye of Round roast."

"Love it." She tapped her foot on the barstool's cross-support, thinking that any second he was going to start divulging details, but instead he continued shuffling around the kitchen—stirring the simmering green beans, pouring boiled potatoes into a colander—just *piddling* when there was so much she wanted to know—

"Okay!" It burst from her like water from a dam breaking. "Spill it already!"

His eyes flicked up from the potatoes, his face charged. He was messing with her. "You sure you don't want to wait until—"

"Tell me!"

A victorious smile split his handsome face. "We got him."

"What!" she exclaimed.

"We got him. Dead to rights. You were right, Boston. It wasn't Beecher."

She gripped the countertop. "Tell me everything."

His face pursed in a tight smile, he dumped the potatoes back into the pot, set it on the counter and picked up a hand-held masher, pounding away as he spoke. "I called the Chief last night—he wants you to come in first thing tomorrow to give a statement about the attack, by the way—"

"Yeah, yeah—but what *happened*?"

"I gave him the rundown about what happened at your place and what you found out. He spoke to Kendall on the phone this morning. Despite what she may have told you, it sounds like Rheardon crossed a serious line with her. I'm talking felony. One with a long statute of limitations."

"Nooo…"

"Yes. We took her statement at the station, then got in touch with Rheardon who, surprisingly, was more than happy to meet us, at his home, on a Sunday afternoon. We walked in, read him his rights—only as a matter of procedure, of course—"

"Of course."

"—We made nice, chatting briefly about his work history, experiences at the school, this year's football chances—and then hit hard with the loaded questions. 'Have you ever had an inappropriate relationship with a student,' etcetera, etcetera, leveraging the shock factor—"

"Sure—"

"And then we point-blank asked him if he remembered Kendall St. James—Kendall Barnes, back then."

"And he denied everything."

Chris stopped mashing and slowly shook his head. "The opposite. He completely broke down. Bawled. *Like a baby*. Fell to his knees, even. Couldn't stand. We had to help him to the couch."

Dani's mouth dropped open. "You're kidding."

"Not kidding. The guy completely caved. Told us all about Kendall, and at least a dozen other girls he's had relationships with over the last thirteen years."

"I can't believe it." A lightness rushed through her, an odd swirling sensation in her brain, the synapses firing, but not connecting, struggling to process that these words being spoken were actually truth.

"And the guy wouldn't shut up. Said the guilt's been killing him—tormenting him. That he can't stop himself but he's too much of a coward to turn himself in or get help. He actually *thanked* us for catching him."

"And what about Jennifer?" Her heart beat faster.

Chris picked up a stick of butter from the counter and tossed it in with the potatoes. "We didn't ask him yet. We wanted to get him pinned down on the other charges first, didn't want to scare him off with murder talk."

"So then, how do you know it was him and not Dr. Beecher?"

He pointed the masher at her. "We asked him if he had any items—any trophies or evidence—that he kept from these girls, anything that connects him to them. It was a long shot, but the guy's in a sharing mood, you know? We figure maybe he'll just volunteer it."

Dani nodded.

"And if you can believe it, he says, 'I've got photos, notes. Mementos even—hair bands, clips.' So, he shows us this box at the top of his closet, full of stuff. We stopped right there and called in the evidence team. Took them a half hour to get there, but when they finally did, while we've got him cuffed in the front room, they do their thing—and that's when they found it."

"Found what?"

"At the back of the closet shelf—a thick lock of hair, blond, about three inches long, tied together with a white ribbon."

Dani wasn't sure whether she was going to be sick, or start crying in relief. "Jennifer's hair."

"We're having it compared to Jennifer's samples right now, but—"

"It's hers," Dani said, knowing with every fiber of her being that it was true.

"I really think so. We'll have to wait for the DNA results to be sure, but we checked it against the autopsy photographs. It's a perfect match."

Dani's chest heaved as she expelled a trembling breath she hadn't realized she had been holding. Her face was hot and she could feel tears beginning to gather. She brushed them away with the back of her hand. "Sorry, I just...it's been so long." Her self-restraint gave, and she choked back an escaping sob. "I can't believe it's really over. Oh...Dr. Beecher. If this had only happened a week ago—" Another heavier sob cut her off, and she began shaking, her shoulders folding in.

"Hey, hey!" Chris soothed, coming around the island to gather her up in his arms. "Come on now, this is good news. Great news!"

She didn't care that she had known him less than a week. She didn't care that she was a police detective and should be stronger than to break down because of a case. All she cared about was that he was someone to share the weight she had been carrying. Someone who understood.

She looked up at him, her eyelashes wet, and blinked. "Sorry," she whispered. "I don't know what's wrong with me."

"Nothing's wrong with you," he said and, tipping her chin down, kissed her forehead gently and rested his cheek against it. "You're perfect."

A peculiar, faint alarm went off in Dani's head, an inexplicable sense of...wrong rising up in her belly. Dani pulled back gently.

He eyed her warily, as if realizing something was amiss. There was disappointment in his gaze as she broke the connection and looked down at the counter, picked up her glass and sipped.

*What is wrong with me?* she asked herself in the uncomfortable quiet that followed. *I like him!*

*Don't I?*

Then, like the hazy playback of a movie, her conversation with Bailey King at the reunion scrolled through her mind, the muscle memory of the instant, magnetic attraction she had felt for him tickling her insides, and suddenly she knew. It wasn't that she didn't like Chris. It was just that there was someone else to consider. Her interaction with Bailey had been short, but electric, and something she wanted to explore, because even for those few minutes, she had experienced a very real sense of connection. And for her, that was rare.

She wasn't one for stringing people along, or allowing misconceptions to persist for convenience's sake, and that's what it felt like was happening here with Chris. This felt too intimate for where she saw them at this point. It was her fault, losing it like that, but she wouldn't do it again. She liked him too much to make more out of their relationship than it was at that moment. It was too much too fast.

"Did I do something wrong?" Chris asked.

"What? No, no," she said, looking up and smiling. "You've been such a good friend to me while I've been here, Chris—"

At the word 'friend,' his mouth turned down. "I was hoping that maybe you'd consider being more than that. I know you live way up north, Boston, but that's not insurmountable," he said, his eyes darkening in intensity as he locked onto hers.

"No, it's not. But...Chris, we just met. I'm not saying no, I'm just saying—"

A frantic knock sounded at the front door, followed by a double ringing of the doorbell. A flash of impatient annoyance passed across Chris's gaze, then he strode from Dani to answer the door.

"Officer Newton, I need your help—I'm so sorry to bother you—" A woman in her early sixties in a loose T-shirt and leggings stood in the doorway. Her gaze flitted to Dani then back to Chris. "I see you've got company, but it's my neighbors again. They're fighting and I think I heard glass shatter. Can you come? I'm worried someone's hurt in there, but I don't want to call 9-1-1 again."

Chris sniffed loudly, his hands on his hips. "Sure, Beverly. I'll come check it out," he said, his voice low and impassive. But when he looked back at Dani, his eyes were pleading. "I'll just be a minute, okay? Will you stick around till I get back?"

"Of course, I will! I'm not going anywhere," she answered, her heart pinching at the thought that she had made him question whether she would stay. She didn't want to leave. She just wanted to slow things down.

At her affirmation his face lightened a bit, and he followed the woman out into the hall.

Alone in the condo, Dani took another sip of water. She breathed in deeply.

*We found him, Doc. We found Jennifer's murderer.*

Regret punched her insides, thinking about how bad the timing was, how they had only missed freeing him by days. Sure, it would've taken some time to get him out of prison, but with DNA evidence and a confession, which they were sure to get with the lock of hair, it wouldn't have been long.

"I'm so sorry," she said, raising her gaze to the ceiling. "I wish I'd been quicker with this."

But she knew he wouldn't have been angry about it. A man like that, especially a man with the kind of faith he had found, would have just been glad that the truth had finally come out. That his children would know their father was innocent.

*I promise, they'll know. The whole world will know. I'll make sure of it.*

The smell of something burning tore her from her thoughts. She sniffed, zeroing in on the oven.

"The rolls!" she exclaimed, and jumped off the stool. Flinging open the oven door, she saw that the bottom edges of the rolls had begun to blacken. She spun in a circle, looking for a pot holder, but instead spotted a towel atop a cutting board. She grabbed it and cried out, yanking her hand back.

A shiny chopping knife had been resting beneath the towel, hidden from view. It had opened a long slice in the skin along the inside of Dani's ring finger on her right hand. Blood began to seep from the cut, slowly at first and then copiously, drops hitting the floor. She grabbed the towel again, wrapped it tightly around the wound, then used it as a holder to remove the pan from the oven. After dropping the pan on the counter, she slammed the oven shut and pulled the towel back to examine her finger. The moment she removed the pressure, the bleeding increased. She rewrapped it.

*Bandages,* she thought. Knowing the bathroom was the likely spot for them and wanting to avoid bleeding on anything else, she ignored the incredible invasion of privacy this was going to amount to and sprinted down the hallway leading to the rest of the condo. When a search of the hall bathroom turned up no bandages, she reluctantly continued to the bedroom at the end.

*Bingo.*

This was the master, and obviously the room Chris used. The bed was unmade, a navy towel hung over a side chair, and a pair of running shoes lay discarded on the rug. She walked straight through to the master bath, and after first unsuccessfully searching under the sink, she found a box of bandages and peroxide on a shelf in the linen closet.

The cut was beginning to ache, even more so as she ran cold water over it, then peroxide to clean it. Selecting the largest of the bandages, she gingerly pulled off her mother's wedding band—she'd been wearing it since the funeral—and awkwardly wrapped the bandage around the two-inch wound. It wasn't pretty—the sticky-side of the bandage had stuck to itself in places, so the end result wasn't smooth—but at least it was tight and contained the bleeding.

Crestfallen, she examined the towel. This man had supported her unwaveringly, even made her dinner for good-ness' sake, then she had gone and hurt his feelings, ruined his towel, *and* let the bread burn.

*I'm the worst.*

She rinsed as much blood out of the towel as she could and left it to soak in the sink, picked her ring up off the counter and walked back into the bedroom, headed for the kitchen. Hoping to force the ring back over the bandage so she wouldn't misplace it, she started to slide it on—and dropped it.

"No!" she exclaimed, unsuccessfully scrabbling for it as it hit the wood floor and rolled noisily across it, disappearing beneath the queen-sized bed that was pushed against the wall opposite the door. "Seriously!" she exclaimed, huffing as she dropped to her knees and lifted the grey, box-pleated bed skirt to peer beneath it.

Nothing. She flicked the overhead light on, then crawled down to look again, tucking the bed skirt under the mattress to allow light to better spill into the space. No ring. A stack of several books, a clear plastic bin of shoes, a longer clear bin with sweaters, and a lot of dust. But no ring.

*Must've rolled somewhere behind all that.*

Trying not to imagine what Chris would think if he walked in and found her there, she hurriedly dragged out both bins and the pile of books. Ducking under again, she finally spotted the ring, lying as far back as possible, against the baseboard near the leg at the head of the bed frame. Slithering beneath the box spring, she stretched out, clasped her fingers around the gold piece, then scooted back out.

With a very intentional, steady hand, she slid the ring down her finger and over the bandage. It was a little too tight, but at least it wasn't going anywhere. She sighed, still sitting on the floor, her mouth turning down as she noticed the dust bunnies scattered across her blouse. After brushing them off as best she could, she pushed the bins back under the bed, then the books —old textbooks by the look of them—until she picked up the last one and stopped.

It was a photograph album, the 8 x 10 sort, leather bound and quite full.

*I shouldn't look.*

But, baby pictures...come on. Maybe Chris in elementary— or high school? She smiled at the thought of what he must have looked like back then. Was he a handsome jock or a bit of an awkward geek like her?

A quick peek couldn't hurt.

She flipped the first page open. Yep, they were baby pictures, adhered to the sticky pages of the album and protected by a clear plastic overlay. A fat, dark-haired baby with ruddy cheeks and curls. She could see the promise of Chris's adult features in the toddler's pudge. A woman snuggled him close.

*His mother? Probably.*

There were several other photos like it, but none depicting a father figure. She turned the next page to find elementary school photos, Chris with missing teeth, one with Santa. She turned more pages, revealing lots and lots of photos with his mother: at home, during holidays, dressed up, but still no father. *They must be close,* she thought. *Or must have been, if she's not alive.* She suddenly felt rather selfish, realizing that she had been so consumed with herself over the last few days, she had never asked about Chris's family.

Junior high and high school photos followed, including pictures from a few dances—one of Chris with a girl on his arm, posing beneath a "Homecoming 1996" banner. Then Chris in a basketball uniform, and action shots taken mid-play.

Another page. A photo of a teenaged girl, maybe fourteen or fifteen, stared out at Dani. It had been taken from a distance, when the girl wasn't looking at the camera. She was pretty, slight, with a fair complexion and the hint of a smile as she stared off somewhere to the right of the frame. There were other similar photos—the girl at a restaurant, at a football game, in a school hallway.

*Maybe she was his girlfriend?* But there were no pictures of them together.

*Maybe she was someone he wished had been his girlfriend, but who had not felt the same way.* Dani had a friend like that in college. The boy had been a dear friend to her, but wanted a different kind of relationship, having feelings she did not reciprocate. The girl and Chris must have at least been friends, because at the bottom of the right page, beneath the clear overlay that protected the photos was a movie stub, dated December 17, 1994, for *Miracle on 34$^{th}$ Street,* from the Archway Theater Movieplex in St. Louis. It was sweet, really, that he had kept this. Teen crushes were so fervent and consuming. She had had her own in Bailey King—which apparently, to her surprise, still had legs—and even had a few keepsakes of her own from those days: a dried corsage and a score card from their first date at putt-putt golf—now both packed away in one of the "Me" boxes.

Her gaze trailed down the page, coming to rest on something below the photos at the bottom: a few short strands of hair, blond by the looks of it, wrapped together by a folded piece of clear tape.

A chill rippled across Dani's skin, but she knew why and dismissed it. They had just been talking about the lock of Jennifer's hair found with Rheardon's things. This little keepsake of Chris's just hit too close to home, that's all. An odd coincidence, at the wrong time.

*Still,* she thought, *it's a bit creepy.* Had the girl given it to him? Had he playfully pulled it from her when she wasn't looking or found it on her brush or jacket? There were legitimate explanations, but still, her nerves tingled uneasily. All of it together—the voyeuristic nature of the photos, the single movie stub, the hair—suggested to the detective in her that there may have been an unhealthy obsession at work.

She turned the page and, thankfully, found no more pictures of the girl, but rather a plethora of family ones. Chris with his mother at an amusement park and on the beach, laughing as a wave hit them. A few older people, presumably grandparents, at a birthday party, with Chris helping an elderly man blow out candles. And in the top right, one of Chris, sandwiched between a man and woman standing on the porch of a white house with green shutters—

Dani gasped.

*I know that house.*

*I know those people.*

This was the caretakers' house at the rear of Dr. Beecher's property. The Pitts' house. And those people, the man and the woman...they were Mr. and Mrs. Pitts.

Why was Chris in a photo with these people? He had never mentioned anything about them. Not in all the time they'd been talking about the case—

Dani ripped back the plastic overlay, peeled the photo from the sticky page beneath, and flipped it over.

*Chris, Uncle Rodney and Aunt Marla, June '95.*

Dani released the photo as if it had burned her, letting it fall to the page where it landed right-side up. Nausea swelled in her gut, her heart thundering as the meaning of those written words sank in.

*Uncle Rodney. Aunt Marla. June '95.*

He didn't just know them. He was related to them. And he had been there *that* summer. With the Pitts. In that house. On that property. Where she found Jennifer...

*Jennifer.*

But he had never said one word.

*You know why.*

Dani wanted to vomit, pass out, scream—a roaring filled her ears, making it difficult to think as she sucked in breath after breath, her lungs heaving, her chest on fire. Why couldn't she breathe? Why couldn't she get enough air?

*Because the migrant worker wasn't a migrant worker at all. It was their nephew, Chris.*

She flung the next page over and her heart all but stopped.

On the left side was a newspaper clipping from the Skye Gazette, dated July 10, 1995. The article's headline read, "Local Girl Murdered," and included Jennifer's sophomore yearbook photo—Jennifer, with her wavy blond hair and happy blue eyes, smiling out at Dani, oblivious to the tragic destiny racing toward her.

Dani's gaze drifted down over the photo and story, to the bottom right corner of the page.

There, tucked protectively beneath the clear plastic, taped into place so as not to slip out, was a small, silver band of twisted vines.

Then the world went black.

## 25

usty, dank earth. Rotting wood and wet decay. And...the taste of blood. She licked her lips, her tongue seeking out the wetness.

*I'm bleeding. Why am I bleeding?*

Dani blinked. It was so dark, everything in shades of black and brown and grey. It had to be late. How much time had passed?

*And where am I?*

Her brain was mud and a vicious ache pounded at the back of her head, rippling out to consume her entire skull. She shut her eyes tightly against it, then blinked again several times. She was facing a wall. And lying on the floor. A wood floor, but not smooth and polished like Chris's condo.

*Chris.*

His name was a shot of adrenaline, cutting through the murkiness, the words of her academy instructor flying back to her: *"Control the situation or the situation will control you."*

*Assess the situation, Danielle.*

She was on the floor, face toward the wall, her hands free.

She was bleeding from the mouth and, given the monster headache, probably from her head too.

*Get up. Now!*

She rolled over and scrambled to her feet, and though all was shrouded in shadow, she knew immediately where she was.

The shed. In the very same corner where she used to hide as a child. And in the diagonally opposite corner, barely illuminated by the faint moonlight dripping through the sparse holes in the roof, stood Chris.

"Don't try anything. I'm armed and you're not." His voice was different. Broken, somehow. She strained to see where his weapon was—held or tucked somewhere—but couldn't make it out. "You've been asleep for hours," he said. "You're pretty when you sleep."

"What...happened, Chris?" A drop of blood trailed down her lip and her hand flew to it, the spot stinging at her touch.

"You hit your face on the corner of the bed frame when you fell." He wiped at his own mouth, as if he were the one bleeding, not her. "Didn't mean for that to happen."

The gnawing ache at the back of her head, somewhere high above her left ear, intensified. She reached a hand to it, finding her hair a moist, matted nest. She pulled her hand back, the blood on it black in the darkness.

"How did we get here?"

He sighed and the sound was beyond sad; it was bereft. A lament, thick with great loss. "This could have been so perfect."

She forced herself to think, to process his words. "What are you talking about?" she asked, backing farther into the corner, pressing herself against the wall.

"You're the last person I would have expected to violate someone's privacy," he said, raw disappointment twisting his features.

"I'm sorry," she whispered. "I didn't mean to. I just...I

needed a bandage." She splayed her wounded hand out so he could see it. "And then my ring rolled under the bed and I found the album. I was just curious about the photos—you know, what you looked like when you were younger—"

"You wanted...you were interested in me?" Squinting, she could make out that his expression had shifted. Eased. What she had said had pleased him.

"Of course, Chris." She worked to keep her tone gentle, warm—though every muscle in her body was aching to let loose a war-cry and take a run at him. "I wasn't snooping. I just...happened on it."

He exhaled wearily.

"Chris, what happened? How did I get here?"

"You don't remember?" he asked quietly.

Dani shook her head. It hurt, and she ceased mid-shake.

"I found you looking at the album. Looking at *her* page. You shouldn't have been." His voice modulated, adopting a far-off, dreamy quality. "You ruined everything, Boston. It could have been so perfect..."

"Chris—"

The sound of his name seemed to bring him back to himself and, as if rattling off a list of meaningless errands he'd undertaken, he spouted, "I hit you to stop you. You fell. When you woke up, you were dazed. I needed to get you out, so I waited awhile, then took you to my car, and drove here. I had to carry you from the car, though. You passed out again by the time we got here."

Bits and pieces of it flashed in Dani's mind. Coming to on his bedroom floor, the cold wood against her cheek. Stumbling to his car, his arm around her waist, holding her up. The dizziness. Falling into his back seat. "People will have seen," she said.

"I doubt it. I didn't leave until after midnight and you were mobile, just unstable. It looked like you were drunk. And that's what I'll tell them. That you drank too much, and I drove you home. Tomorrow, when you don't come back for your car, I'll call you, and eventually get Sasha involved."

"You'll be a suspect. You'll be the last person to have seen me."

"You've had break-ins, remember? Someone is after you. They'll be the target, not me."

"But my blood is at your place."

"And you cut your hand. Easily explained," he countered.

*No. Not easily explained.* It was a terrible plan with a million holes in it that she could see, even in her dazed state. But he was apparently blind to them and continued confidently laying out his scheme.

"I'll say we were looking at old photos in my bedroom and you split your hand open again. I'll have to take their photos and keepsakes out of the album first, but that's easy enough."

*The ring in the album.* "You have Jennifer's ring, Chris."

His face dropped. "I needed to keep it. I needed it to keep her close. Just like her lock of hair. But I had to leave that at Rheardon's. The ring is all I have now."

*You have to keep him talking*, her training whispered to her. *Get it all out.*

"Tell me, Chris. Tell me what happened to Jennifer. Please."

A shadow, darker than the ones cloaking the space fell across his countenance. "She was so very disappointing. She ruined everything. Just like you."

He was all over the place. She had to corral him, guide him.

"Chris—the photo with your aunt and uncle. You came from St. Louis to stay with them that summer?"

"As soon as school was out. I didn't want to come. I wanted to stay home with my mom. But she made me come."

"Why?"

"Because of her." For several beats he looked up at the roof, as if trying to see the sky through one of the holes. Then his gaze fell back on Dani. "You saw her. In the album."

*The girl in the pictures.* Dani nodded. "Who is she?"

"Kayla."

"Why did you have to leave because of Kayla?"

"She was so beautiful." His eyelids fell and a strange, almost angelic peace settled in his features as he focused on whatever images he was conjuring. "Flowing blond hair—nearly white it was so blond—and her eyes..." He opened his, focusing on Dani again. "They were blue. Big and blue. So big you could get lost in them."

Suddenly his body went rigid, the illusion of peace shattered, his voice now somewhat robotic. "I had to leave because Mom knew. I'd told her how I felt about Kayla. We used to tell each other everything. She helped me work up the nerve to speak to Kayla and ask her out. It was just a stupid dance, but Kayla laughed at me and..." He trailed off, shame clouding his gaze. "Mom caught me crying about it and I told her what Kayla had done. How she laughed...I shouldn't have, I shouldn't have told her anything but I couldn't help it. So when they found her, Mom knew."

*When they found her.* Ice cold fear swirled inside Dani. "Chris," she said, her heart pounding against her ribs. "What did your mom know?"

His brow furrowed. "That I'd killed her, of course." He snorted. "Come on, you're sharper than that, Boston."

For a second, he sounded like the Chris that had shown up at her house with a supreme pizza and laughed with her about foul-ups on the job. But that Chris had never really existed. It had always been this Chris in disguise. The one with an album under his bed that contained photographs of two dead girls, stolen strands of hair and a ring of twisted vines taken from the corpse of her friend.

"Mom never said it outright, but she knew," he plowed on. "She'd seen the pictures and the hair—you saw the hair, right?"

Without stopping to think about whether she should or not, Dani nodded.

"Mom was afraid. Afraid someone would figure it out. So she sent me away." His voice grew sour. "I didn't want to go. I wanted to be near Kayla. I wanted to go to her funeral and touch her one last time before they put her in the ground." He gingerly ran a finger in midair along a surface that wasn't there. "I wanted to tell her I still loved her. Whisper it over her...but Mom sent me here and I never got the chance."

"She sent you to stay with the Pitts?"

He nodded. "Mom's sister and her husband."

"But, Chris, how is it that no one ever saw you? *I* never saw you and I rode my bike through there all the time—"

"They didn't want anyone to see me. So I stayed in the back fields, mostly. Didn't want any questions about me or why I was there. Mom was terrified that if I stayed in St. Louis, I'd do something that would draw attention to myself in the investigation. But she was also paranoid that my absence from St. Louis might be a red flag—apparently the police were interviewing everyone who knew Kayla. Even though we were in the same grade, I didn't 'know' her that way. And Kayla never got a chance to tell anyone that I had asked her out and she'd turned me down. So unless they had a reason to suspect me—like me skipping town—the cops wouldn't even look at me.

"So, Mom made Aunt Marla promise to keep my visit quiet, because I was 'troubled,'" he punctuated the words with air-quotes, "and didn't want me agitated with a lot of questions. They told Dr. Beecher and anybody else that might have caught sight of me that I was some 'migrant worker' they were helping out, and that was that. Plus, I think they were afraid."

"Afraid of what?"

"Of me. Of letting me around other people. I think Mom

must have told Aunt Marla about Kayla at some point. Aunt Marla insisted that I keep to myself, and that was fine with me. I didn't want anybody anyway. Kayla was the only one for me. Until I saw *her*." He looked transported again.

"Jennifer?" Dani asked.

"Jennifer." He sighed, his shoulders rising and falling contentedly. "She was an angel, walking down by the river with that blond hair—the same as Kayla—coming down over her shoulders." He ran his hands over his head, smoothing imaginary locks of hair. "It gleamed like gold when the sun hit it just right in the afternoon. Just like gold." He seemed to realize Dani was watching him, and his mood sobered. "After that first time, I brought binoculars with me to the field when I was working so I could see her without her seeing me. I got as close as I could, hiding behind trees and bushes...day after day she played with those kids, walking down to the river and back. For weeks, I just watched."

"And then what?" Her words were barely a whisper, afraid anything more might shut him down.

"I studied her. I *sensed* her. And finally I realized that Kayla —Kayla had just been an image of what was supposed to be and that Jennifer was the real one. *The* one. And then—" without warning, a savage hatred corrupted his handsome features with such ferocity that Dani pressed harder into the wall just to get farther away from him, "—and then I saw her, meeting *him*, in that shed," he growled.

"Who?" Dani asked, though she thought she knew who he meant.

*Jennifer's mystery boyfriend, Peter.*

"I never knew. I didn't get a good look at his face. But I could see hers and I could tell she loved him and, oh," he actually choked back a sob, "it broke me again. The same way Kayla had broken me. And I knew I had to do something. Something before I lost her. It took a while to work up my nerve, but then, that day—she must have just gotten off work because it was later in the afternoon—I was in the field and saw her go to the shed. Alone. I was so excited, because I knew it was my chance. I followed her inside and when she turned around to see me, she was so happy, smiling so wide..."

His own mouth split in a grin as his eyes closed again, likely resurrecting more memories of Jennifer. Then the grin vanished, replaced by sheer contempt as his eyes shot open, his gaze hard as steel. "Until she realized it was me, not him. She yelled at me, asking who I was and why was I there and what did I want—I tried to calm her down, I told her that I was there because we belonged together." Urgent desperation drove his words now, as he ran his hands through his hair, pacing back and forth. "I said I wanted her to know me and love me, because I loved her—and she got quiet at that, but I could see she was terrified. I told her she didn't have to be afraid of me, but she shoved me out of the way and ran, yelling, 'Get away from me! Get away!'"

Suddenly he stopped moving, grew eerily statue-still, and twisted his head slightly as if tuning in to the distant memory. "I caught her then, grabbed her arm right before she reached the honeysuckle bush. I yanked her back, and when she turned I could see the disgust in her eyes. It was the same way Kayla had looked at me, right before she laughed. But I wasn't going to let Jennifer laugh. Because I wasn't going to let her ruin it. Because she was the one, my forever one, and if she laughed, that would have ruined it. So I made it so she couldn't laugh." He expelled a breath in relief. "I made it forever perfect."

"You killed her."

His face hardened. "I *preserved* her. I saved her from making the biggest mistake of her life. And now she has been loved perfectly for thirteen years."

"What about the diary, the bracelet—"

"Her things. Her precious things. I took them from her—

she had them all with her that day. The bracelet, the ring, the diary tucked in her waistband—she must've been planning on showing him. I wasn't happy that I had to give up the bracelet to misdirect the police."

"You planted it in Dr. Beecher's nightstand."

"See, Boston, that's how I *knew* it was meant to be because... it just all fit together so easily."

The throbbing in Dani's head was like a hammer pounding her brain, and she uttered her question through a tight grimace. "What fit together?"

"Earlier in the day, I'd come up the riverbank toward the house, trying to get a look at her inside with the kids. I did that sometimes. I was careful, stayed hidden behind the brush and used the binoculars...but all of the sudden she barreled out of the house, crying, and ran down the gravel road, headed for the riverbank. She was so upset and nearly fell, but Dr. Beecher had followed her, and managed to grab her and keep her from falling when she slipped. So, afterwards, I remembered that and thought—make him the scapegoat. It was easy. No one was home—they'd all gone out. I popped in, put the bracelet in the drawer and popped out.

"I went home and Aunt Marla caught me washing her blood out of my shirt. I said it was mine, but she wasn't stupid. I didn't have any cuts and somehow she just *knew* something had gone wrong. I think it was because Uncle Rodney had caught me watching Jennifer a week earlier and warned me off. Aunt Marla didn't know what had happened, but she knew it was something bad. Uncle Rodney drove me to Birmingham that night and put me on a bus back to St. Louis. You found Jennifer the next day."

"And no one knew you had ever been here."

He shook his head. "The migrant worker just disappeared."

"How convenient," Dani muttered.

"I know, right? It was proof that it was meant to be. Just like you were meant to be." There was a disturbing shift in his aspect as he laser-focused on her.

"Me?"

"You're not being a very good detective, Boston." He bent his head toward her. "And I need you to understand. It's important that you understand."

"Fine. You want me to play detective? Then tell me why you came back here, Chris? You'd gotten away with it. You were in the clear. Why move back to Skye?"

Disappointment creased his face. Apparently he still felt like she wasn't getting it. "Jennifer was *the* one. So as soon as I could, as soon as a position opened up, I came back to be close to her." He stepped a few feet nearer Dani, spreading his arms wide. She could see that his weapon wasn't in either hand, nor did she see a holster, meaning it was probably tucked into his waistband behind his back.

"This is the place I spoke to her. Professed my love to her. This is my special sanctuary." He squatted down and patted the place where Dani had found the diary. The original floorboard was gone, but the crime scene investigator had left a loose, larger board over the space, presumably to avoid creating a safety hazard. "And here, here is where I kept the heart of her— her diary—in my sanctuary, the place I'd known with her." He sat back on his haunches and looked up at Dani. "I've sat here and read it a million times. Nearly memorized it. Every word. Every sweet word."

He closed his eyes and Dani wondered if he was seeing Jennifer's flowery scrawl across the pages of her private recollections and dreams.

"What did you mean a minute ago, when you said, 'just like I was meant to be'?" she asked. The question seemed to register slowly with him, until a smile broke out on his face, and he rose to his full height, opening his eyes to take her in again.

"For the last six years I've been coming here, walking through that deserted property, down that gravel road to this dilapidated shed to unearth Jennifer's heart and pour over it, to profess my love for her again and again. Six years, living out a shadow of the love that could have been. And then, last week—just a plain old, ordinary week like any other—everything changed. Because of you." His voice rose in pitch. "I walked into Green's Drugs and there you were, impossibly sitting at the counter with Sasha and Peter, with your blond hair and your blue eyes, looking like *her*." He grabbed his chest. "I thought my heart was going to stop. I thought I would fall out right there on the floor."

Dani remembered that day. That moment. She had seen him come in, looking so handsome, and she had—

"You smiled," he said, and adoration beamed from him. "You smiled. At *me*. And I knew. You were *her*. The her she had never become. I thought to myself, *this is it. She is the one.* But then," his expression darkened, "when I left, I doubted everything. I was so confused. I wasn't even sure I had really seen you. I was so overwhelmed, I needed to be *here*. To come sit here, and think and talk to Jennifer. So I came, even though it wasn't my regular night."

His shoulders dropped. "You cannot know the joy I felt when I walked up that riverbank and saw you entering my shed. It was a sign. I watched from the bushes, waited to see— and then you ran out, carrying Jennifer's diary, carrying her very heart and I just knew."

*He is completely insane.* The neurons of Dani's brain were firing at full speed, wildly searching for a way out of the situation that didn't end with her dead.

"I needed to get close to you—to know you better. And I could feel you, there in your house. Touching your things. Imagining you holding them. I left you hints, just so you would know."

She worked to keep her voice even. "Why did you take the diary and the file?"

"Well, you took *my* diary first, and then you gave it to the police." It was an accusation, not an explanation. "I had to do something, because I'd never made a copy—a copy just wouldn't have been the same and I also didn't want to risk someone seeing me with it. Since trying to get the original or Dr. Beecher's copy back from the police would've been too risky, I had to settle for your copy. And I took the file because it would seem odd for an intruder interested in Jennifer's diary to leave her murder file behind. Unless he already had access to the file, and I definitely didn't want anyone to start thinking like that."

*Dr. Beecher's copy.* Her heart lurched at the thought of Dr. Beecher taking the fall for Chris. "He was innocent, Chris. An innocent man. And you let him go to prison and die because of your lies." Fire burned in her belly, and though she knew she shouldn't antagonize him—that she should be sympathizing and empathizing and establishing rapport—she just didn't care.

"No, Boston," he corrected slyly, "you're the one that let him die. I warned you. We all warned you—the Chief, your friends —to leave well enough alone. But you didn't. You passed the diary on to Beecher and that couldn't be allowed."

Sick realization made her suck in a quivering breath. "You had him killed?"

"You left me no choice."

"But you knew there wasn't anything in the diary that he could use against you. You said yourself that you read it a million times—"

"There was nothing that pointed to me directly. Nothing within my scope of knowledge that seemed dangerous to me, but I had no idea what Beecher would see in it, what knowledge he would bring to it that might help him prove his case.

Would it jog his memory? Unearth a conflicting story he hadn't known about before? Would it provide him with anything, anything at all, that would make the authorities take a second look at his case? Because I couldn't risk that. I couldn't *allow* that. Because if people started digging, they just might uncover me. But if Beecher was dead, not only would he be unable to provide insight on the diary passages, there would be no reason to pursue a review of his case. Problem solved."

*He's going to kill me.* And time was running out. She could see it in his eyes.

Chris Newton was completely out of touch with reality, and had already killed two—*no, three people*—she corrected herself, thinking of Kayla in St. Louis. If she stayed in this shed with him, she was going to end up dead. Because now she knew the truth, and no matter what she promised, or how she plied him with hopes of some kind of twisted "love" between them, he wouldn't be able to risk her leaving there and telling someone. She knew it and he knew it.

He started talking about Jennifer again, about how much Dani looked like her now, with her new, fully-blond hair, and how much she reminded him of her. His words faded in her ears as she worked to come up with a plan, a way out. She forced down the panic, the fear, the guilt that was crushing her, and let her training take control. Holding her head still so as not to arouse his suspicion, she cast around in search of some kind of weapon. But there was nothing. The place had been wiped clean when the crime scene investigator came through, taking everything—

*The crime scene investigator.* Her eyes fell on the diary's former resting place as she dialed back into what Chris was muttering.

"...like her. And so now here I am, with another problem that didn't have to be." He paused expectantly, then spoke for her when she offered nothing. "You. You're that problem. Oh,

Boston," he moaned, taking another step back and running his hands wretchedly over his head. "Why? Why couldn't you just have left it? I was there for you. Why wasn't I enough?"

As if the strength had finally been drained from her, she slid down the corner, all the way to the floor. He watched her, the pain in his eyes nearly palpable. If she had to guess, she would say that he truly did not *want* to have to end her. Not that that would stop him. Stretching out so she was on all fours, she crawled toward him, her knees dragging across the wooden planks, tiny splinters catching in the fabric of her pants, scratching her skin.

It wasn't far. A few feet at most until she reached him. She grabbed his ankles, right above his leather topsiders, and bowed her forehead against his feet. "I'm so sorry, Chris," she said, sniffling, her voice catching between words. "I didn't realize. I didn't want to ruin anything."

"Then why?" he asked, and she felt his fingers brush gently across the crown of her head, her face still bent toward the floor. "Why didn't you just let it go?"

"Because I didn't understand. I didn't *see*." Dani dragged one hand from his shoe, and dropped it to the floor, pushing herself up on one arm, still looking down as she heaved a sob. "I get it now. I do."

"But—" he said, and she felt something drop onto her head, then trickle down.

He was *crying*.

"—it's too late, Boston. I don't know what else to do. You've spoiled it. And now I have to preserve you the way I preserved her. Keep you perfect until—"

Wham! In one fluid motion Dani grabbed and sliced upward with the temporary board the crime scene investigator had left behind, contacting violently with the underside of Chris's chin. His head whipped back and he stumbled in reverse as she followed through, jamming the end of the plank into his gut like a battering-ram so that he doubled over. She plowed her body into him, driving him against the wall, but he shoved back, roaring like a wild animal and charging her. Barely still holding on to the plank with one hand, she awkwardly slung it upward with all the strength she could muster, cracking him on the side of the head and dropping him to the floor.

Then she ran.

# 26

Dani bobbled unsteadily as she ran from the shed, her own feet nearly tripping her more than once as she sprinted over the uneven earth. Behind her, the shed door crashed open, and she turned to see it bang into the exterior wall so hard that it broke a hinge, leaving it sagging as Chris stumbled out. He swiveled frantically, searching...then froze as their gazes connected. His head dipped slightly, as if locking in a target, then he moved, his rough, staggered paces taking a direct route toward her.

Dani stepped backward, one quick stride after another, but he kept coming, his heavy, pounding footfalls bringing him nearer, nearer, until she knew that delaying any longer would close the distance between them.

So she halted, facing him, and though still yards away, he stopped abruptly, confusion gilding his stare. Blood dripped down his forehead, a dark stain running into one eyebrow.

"You stopped."

She shrugged. "I can't outrun you."

He shook his head. "No. You can't." A faint smile curved his mouth. "Look where we are."

They were standing somewhere along the spread of the honeysuckle bush, the night turning its leafy mounds a deep blackish-green and its flowers into faint glimmers in the moonlight. "We're back where it all started. Do you see now?" he asked in earnest. "Do you see how this was *meant* to be? You found her here, and now you'll be found here and together we will share that always." He stepped toward her.

"Don't," Dani said. Her voice was forceful. All traces of the weak, pleading woman in distress had vanished. "Don't come any closer."

A flicker of adoration stole across his face. "You're stronger than the others, Boston. You're more like me. We would have made such a pair," he said, and reached behind his back, his hand grasping—then shock rolled over his visage as Dani planted her feet in a shooting stance, leveling his gun at his center mass.

"I mean it, Chris. I don't want to shoot you, but I will." She measured each word, carving them out so that they were steady and sure, leaving no room for him to question her resolve, even though her head was on fire, her legs were starting to shake and the edges of her vision were beginning to dim.

His face drained, stark white against the night. "I didn't even feel you take it off me."

"You were dazed."

And that was it. He sank slowly, crumpling down onto the dry earth. He pulled his knees up to his chest and wrapped his arms around them, rocking like a child attempting to self-soothe. "It was going to be so perfect," he whispered, his voice barely audible. "Finally."

"Give me your phone, Chris."

She held out her hand, but instead of complying, he submissively rolled onto his side, facing away from her and exposing the bulge of the phone in his back pocket. Cautiously she edged forward, her nerves on alert, ready to pull the trigger if he so much as flinched.

But he didn't. He just lay there, rolled into a ball.

The handsome detective—the clever, jovial man she had welcomed into her world, borne her heart to, even considered taking a risk on, was no more. The facade had been peeled away and this broken, withered shell was all that was left. With the gun trained on him, she extended her other hand, keeping as much distance as she could between them, and slipped his cell out of his pocket. Quickly backpedaling out of his reach, she dialed 9-1-1. After requesting assistance, she left the line open, slipped the cell into her pants pocket, and returned both hands to the weapon's grip, aiming the muzzle squarely at the back of Chris's head.

"Chris Newton, I'm placing you under arrest for the murders of Jennifer Cartwright and Thomas Beecher. You have the right to remain silent. Anything you say can, and will, be used against you in a court of law..."

## 27

The next few days were a whirlwind of doctor's visits—she had, in fact, sustained a concussion—police interviews and media calls, meeting with Jennifer's parents, speaking to Dr. Beecher's ex-wife and children, and packing. So, so much packing. But finally, the day before, on Wednesday afternoon, Estate Settlers had shown up and begun coordinating the disposal of the trash, the charity collection of the donation boxes, and the loading up of everything else to be hauled off to Birmingham to be sold online or at auction.

Now, it was Thursday morning, and the last Estate Settlers' truck had finally pulled out of the driveway an hour ago. Dani sat on the front porch—it was the only place to sit now that the furniture was gone—with Peter and Sasha flanking her. Perched on the steps like they had done so often during their teen years, it almost felt like they were there again.

Almost.

They each cradled a cup of coffee, brought by Sasha from Green's Drugs, since Dani's father's coffee and brewer had already been shipped to Boston in one of the "Me" boxes. At ten in the morning it was already too hot to be drinking coffee outside, but Dani kept sipping. She needed all the caffeine she could get to make it through this long travel day, even if it did mean sucking down the blistering liquid in ninety-degree weather.

Together they stared out at the poplar trees on opposite ends of the front yard, green and full, their shade covering most of the grass, keeping the fescue happy and green as well. The trio had been there for nearly half an hour, but Peter and Sasha hadn't said much. What was there for someone to say in moments like that—when such a monumental shift occurs in your life, it's as if the actual tectonic plates beneath you have realigned, but you're the only one that feels it? Four lives— Dani's included—had been wrapped up in that house. Tears and joys and disappointments and victories...and just like that, it was all gone. Wiped clean. Now someone else would make memories there. It would be the center of someone else's universe.

"And you're sure all your stuff's been shipped? You don't need me to send anything?" Sasha asked.

Dani shook her head. "Nope. You saw how cleaned out it was in there."

"It's bizarre," Peter said. "Just doesn't feel right without your parents' things inside."

"Don't you need it staged with something?" Sasha asked. "I could bring a few things over—"

"Thanks, but no," Dani said. "The agent's handling it. She's got a staging company coming in next week, but honestly, we may not even need it. She told me she's had two serious inquiries since she posted the house online yesterday. She thinks it'll sell in days."

"Well, I hope so. For your sake," Peter said, bumping shoulders with Dani. "It's hard when these things drag on."

"Yeah." She looked at him and could feel the mutual understanding pass between them once again. In all the statements,

*Secrets She Knew*

interviews and questioning, she hadn't mentioned anything about him being Jennifer's mystery boyfriend. And she never would. Chris had confessed. There was no point in dragging Peter through the mud just for the sake of outing every inch of the truth.

He tossed her a meaningful smile, ripe with gratitude, and she nodded, just in case he needed the reassurance of her silence one last time.

"I just can't believe I was so wrong about him," Sasha spouted out of nowhere. It had been like this ever since Chris's arrest. They would be talking about something else altogether, or quietly working, and out of the blue Sasha would pipe up, apologizing for trying to set Dani up with him and for being what she called, "such a shoddy judge of character." She would wring her hands and shake her head, berating herself. "I don't know how I missed it. He was just so—"

"Sasha, seriously. Stop it," Dani said, putting a hand on Sasha's knee to halt the tirade. "It wasn't just you. He had everyone fooled. Including the Chief. Including *me*," Dani said, patting her chest. "I want this to be the last time you apologize, got it?"

"But I gave you something to hope for, Dani. I could see how he looked at you—"

"It was never going to work out with me and Chris, Sash."

Sasha's brow wrinkled, exposing a single line between her eyebrows. "What?"

"I mean, yeah, he was really handsome and we had the detective thing in common, and he was funny and interesting, but...there was just something that didn't quite fit. I could never really put my finger on it, but I just had a feeling. My spidey-senses, you know? There were times when something about him, I don't know, just...bothered me. Times he was oddly protective—too soon, too concerned, even a little bossy about it —I shrugged it off, chalking it up to just normal friendly

201

concern, and maybe his detective mindset, but now it makes sense. I never reached a point where I was ready to pursue anything with him. So you pushing us together didn't scar me."

"Promise?"

"Promise," Dani answered, prompting Sasha to throw her arm around her and hug her tightly. "But I want you to take this as a sign and *stop trying to set people up.* You absolutely stink at it."

"Yeah, you really do," Peter chimed in, an amused twist to his lips.

Genuine disbelief saturated Sasha's countenance. "What? I put you and Amy together—"

"No," Peter corrected, "You set me up with Amy's sister, remember?"

Sasha's eyes narrowed, then relaxed. "Oh, right."

"So, let me find my own dates, please," Dani said, leaning into her friend playfully.

"But you won't," Sasha whined. "You'll go back to Boston and back to your job and it'll be the same old grind again—"

"Shows what you know," Dani remarked, injecting a sizable dose of mystery into her tone.

Interest curled Sasha's lip as she leaned back and appraised Dani. "What are you talking about?"

"Bailey King," Dani said, and despite her attempts to hide it, she was sure the satisfaction of surprising Sasha with this little tidbit was showing on her face.

Sasha's gaze shot to Peter. "Did you know about this?"

Peter held his hands up, laughing. "Uh, no. Not me. First I'm hearing."

"So," Sasha exclaimed impatiently, elbowing Dani, "spill it!"

Dani held her tongue for a minute, allowing the suspense to build. The look on Sasha's face was priceless. Finally she relented. "I've got a date with him, in Boston a week from tonight."

"Nooooooo," Sasha drawled. "How—"

"He came here yesterday, after you left. Said he'd heard about everything with Chris and Jennifer's case and all—how could he not, with it all over the news—but he wanted to wait until the frenzy died down just a bit, to reach out and make sure I was okay."

"Nooooooo," Sasha repeated.

Dani nodded. "He asked if I would consider dinner in Boston when I got back. I told him I would."

Sasha clapped her hands together, while Peter cocked his head. "You sure, Dani?"

"Yeah," she said. "Why?"

He pursed his lips before answering. "I don't know. It's just... it's not like you to move so fast. I mean, I know you said you already knew Chris wasn't your Prince Charming, but you were still sort of, I don't know, interested in him and you've just been through so much in the past week—"

"I'm done living in the past." She meant it as a response to his comment, but she also meant it as a resolution in general. "I've let my past in this place and its tragedies—Jennifer's and Dr. Beecher's—define me for far too long. But," she sucked in a breath and straightened her shoulders, feeling a surprising sense of strength in actually saying it out loud, "the ghosts have been put to rest, and I think it's time for me to move on too. I'm not taking any of it back with me, including Chris Newton. I want a fresh start. I want to define myself, my purpose, by something more hopeful."

"Like what?" Sasha asked, but the spark in her eye told Dani that she too remembered their conversation at the sink on Sunday.

"I've got some ideas," Dani replied, gracing her friend with a warm smile.

"You're not *exactly* leaving the past behind, really, though, are you?" Peter said with a smirk. "Not when your first step into this brave new world involves dating the first boyfriend you ever had."

"I'm not leaving it all behind. Just the weight I was never meant to carry. The rest of it—the good stuff," she said, linking her arms through theirs, "*that*, I'm never letting go."

## 28

"I'm so sorry, Dani." There was an edge to the Chief's words as he spoke, a cutting regret to match the weary remorse lining his scruffy features as Dani listened from the chair in front of his desk. He leaned forward on the desk blotter, his arms crossed, almost as if he needed the support to keep steady. She had never seen him this shaken.

"It's all right. Really—"

"No. All this time, all these years, you kept saying—you were the *only* one who kept saying—that we'd gotten it wrong. Not a soul bought into it, but you held on just the same. And I'm just so sorry that I wasn't there for you. That I didn't believe it."

"I get it, Chief. It was just a feeling, of a fifteen-year-old girl, no less—"

"You didn't stay fifteen."

"No, but I never had anything real for you to go on. Not until now. I'm just glad it's finally over." Dani shifted in her chair, trying to ignore the lingering, dull headache that had plagued her since Sunday night. She checked her watch. Her next Tylenol dose was overdue. "So where do things stand?" she asked.

Since Monday she had been getting short updates from the Chief, but he had been adamant that he couldn't share much until they were further into the investigation. Now that a few days had passed, and the department had apparently gotten their ducks in a row, he had invited her in for a quick briefing before she headed to Birmingham for her flight back to Boston.

"Well, it's about what you'd expect. Chris blabbed on and on until his lawyer showed up and then he shut down. Hasn't spoken a word to us since, but we've pretty much put the picture together at this point. Jennifer...well, you know about Jennifer, he told you that."

"Yeah." In the shed, Chris had made it very clear exactly what had happened to Jennifer Cartwright.

"That was her ring you found in his album. There were a couple of strands of loose hair there too—we're having them tested—but we suspect he kept Jennifer's lock of hair on that same page before planting it at Rheardon's place with all of Rheardon's other trophies." The Chief's face curdled, and his shoulders sank. "That was a complete disaster too." He snorted. "Right out of a screenplay. Cop on the scene, first to the evidence, has the perfect opportunity to plant something. Contaminates the whole investigation."

"You couldn't have known."

"Well, fortunately Rheardon's already owned up to his inappropriate actions with all those teens, so we really don't need the trophies to make a case. If we did, he could claim that the evidence was tainted. We'd have a hard time nailing him then."

Concern wriggled in Dani's gut. "But you're good? You've got him on those charges?"

"Oh, yeah. He wanted a deal. The D.A.'s working it out now. By the way, we asked Rheardon about Jennifer confronting him and he admitted to that too. We also got an explanation for why Jennifer wrote in the diary that she was afraid no one would believe her if she told someone about Rheardon. Turns out she had a C- average in his class. Would have given her a reason to make up stories about him." He paused. "Speaking of stories, there's an interesting one about the shed."

"Which is?"

"As part of initially securing the warrant to search the shed after you found the diary, we tracked down the property's current owner. Seems that after Dr. Beecher sold the property to the Pitts, and then they both died, it was auctioned off to a holding company in Delaware. That was good enough for the warrant. We didn't need to look any further at that point, so we didn't. But now, with everything that's happened, we thought we should. Guess who owns the holding company."

"Not Chris."

"Right in one," the Chief remarked.

"So that's how he made sure the shed would remain undisturbed and accessible. He bought it."

"Exactly."

She shook her head against the irony of it all. "How utterly convenient for Chris that the Pitts died off, giving him eternal access to that place."

The Chief eyed her warily.

"Oh, he didn't," she said, taking his morbid meaning.

"Well, definitely not the uncle. The boating accident that killed him happened when another local—drunk out of his mind—collided with him. Not something Chris could have been involved in. But the aunt?" He patted a stack of papers to his right. "We're having her body exhumed. She died suddenly of a heart attack seven years ago. At the time, her doctor thought it was odd—she was healthy as a horse—but there was no family and no reason to suspect foul play. Looking at it now, though, given what she knew about Chris's past and the timing of her death in relation to Chris's move here, and his obsessive use of the shed..." He let his sentence hang, the import of the facts obvious.

"Yeah, um, the shed...something I was thinking about—how is it that your crime scene investigator didn't find Chris's prints there if he's been visiting it for years?" Dani asked.

"We asked Chris the same question." The Chief wiggled his fingers. "Said he wore gloves every single time. He might be disturbed, but he isn't stupid. It's also why we didn't find his prints on Jennifer or her bike in 1995. He managed to grab a pair of work gloves from the shed along with a tool of some sort before going after her."

"And Dr. Beecher? How did Chris get to him?"

The Chief's face turned pink and he swallowed hard. If Dani didn't know better, she would have thought he was about to cry. "We're still pinning all that down. But it looks like Chris reached out to someone who had contacts inside the prison to arrange the hit. I can't say any more than that now. The identity of the middleman looks like something Chris might be willing to trade on, and if we get that name, well, that could open up a whole new can of worms." The Chief looked down at his folded hands, keeping his focus there as he rolled his thumbs over each other. "I feel the worst about him—Dr. Beecher. Rotting away in prison, innocent, no one believing him. And then...if he'd just lived one more week."

She knew how he felt—what it was like to have to ask a "what if" question. If she hadn't given the diary to Dr. Beecher, it was possible that Chris might not have felt the need to get rid of him. But she wasn't going to carry that burden and he shouldn't either. Dani reached a hand out across the desk, covering the Chief's interlaced fingers. "Don't do that. Don't do that to yourself. You did the best you could—and you're not the one who killed him. The only person responsible for that is Chris Newton. Don't strap that baggage on. You hear me?"

A weak smile emerged on the Chief's lips. "Yeah. I hear you, Officer Lake."

"Detective," Dani reminded him, returning his smile and wresting a meager, but warm chuckle from her friend.

# 29

---

Dani steered the grey rental sedan out of her parents' neighborhood, turning left at the light.

*This is the last time I'll ever pull out of here after staying in that house, because I'll never stay in that house again.*

The notion pummeled her heart afresh, even though she had been telling herself things like that all day.

*This is the last time you'll wake up here.*

*This is the last time you'll eat here.*

But somehow, with the stone subdivision sign disappearing in the rearview mirror, pulling away from the intersection made it so much more real in a way nothing else had. She sucked in a breath, fighting back sentimental tears.

Her parents didn't live there anymore. Her familial connection to the town was gone. Yes, she would visit. She would come see Sasha and Peter and watch their families grow, and eat cheeseburgers at the counter at Green's...but it wouldn't be the same. A chapter had closed in her personal journey and there would be no reopening it.

The wheels thu-thunked as she crossed the metal threshold onto the Claythorne River bridge, and then again as she left it.

The sound was like a hammer driving nails into the coffin of her former life.

To the west, increasingly dark bands painted the horizon, warning of the strong storms the news had promised would hit in about twenty minutes. Dani would be turning east once she reached the highway, and should have no trouble staying ahead of the deluge, but the storm would be chasing her all the way to Birmingham. In confirmation, lightning struck somewhere far in the distance, lighting up the sky in shades of yellowish-green. The thunder, crashing nearly twenty-five seconds later by her count, assured her that the tempest was still far off enough that she would beat it.

She lowered the window, allowing the robust scent of cut grass and the hot, sticky wind preceding the storm to flow through the cabin. It whipped her hair across her face and she snatched at it, tucking the loose ends securely behind her ears. The air-conditioner would have been more comfortable, but she wanted it like this. She was leaving Skye—at least the Skye that had always had a chokehold on her—and she wanted to feel it blow by as she left it behind. The storm might be chasing her out of town, but this time, unlike every other exit from this place, it would be the *only* thing chasing her. The ghosts had been laid to rest. The questions answered. The secrets unearthed.

Justice done.

For the first time in her life, Dani was leaving Skye unburdened by the belief that she owed it or Jennifer Cartwright or Dr. Beecher anything. She finally had shed the chains she didn't even know were binding her. And now...now she was a free woman.

Dani felt a smile blossom on her face. She was starting over. It was exhilarating and terrifying all at the same time—like a diver, standing on the high board, toes on the edge, ready to leap. And there was a lot to sort out. But there were a couple of things she knew for certain.

The first was that she would continue on as a detective, no question about it—that was in her blood. But as Sasha had pointed out, though that might be what she *did*, it couldn't be who she *was*. Defining herself by that job would only lead to heartache and burnout. There would be no peace found in defining herself by what she did or accomplished, any more than she had found peace rooting her identity in a twisted sense of responsibility and guilt, or her relationship with a person. For years Dani had allowed herself to be defined by all of those—a responsibility to bring Jennifer's murderer to justice, her guilt over setting the wheels in motion that resulted in Dr. Beecher's tragic conviction, and her failed marriage to Finn. But no more. That kind of identity was the very opposite of freedom.

Which led to the second thing. Danielle Lake needed to figure out who she really was—and what *should* define her. The next time the world disappointed, betrayed, fell apart around her—which it inevitably would at some point, because, well, it always does—what of her would be left? At the end of all things, what would define her in such a way that she could stand, survive intact—no matter what, come what may?

To figure that out, she needed to go back to the beginning— examine the person she was before Jennifer Cartwright, and the truths her parents had trusted and see how they might resonate with her now. Sasha seemed to believe these things held the key to unlocking the answers she was seeking, and though the woman was terrible at match-making, she understood Dani better than anyone, even Peter. And if Sasha found that much contentment, that much fulfillment in those same truths—

*Then they're worth considering.*

The new Danielle Lake could remember the events of her

past, but it was time to stop living in and for them. She refused to allow them to steal one more moment of her present or future. She had too much to look forward to—a new career as a detective, hopeful possibilities with Bailey King, and becoming the person she was truly meant to be, instead of the person she had defaulted into.

On her right, a green-and-white sign atop a white wooden post proclaimed, "You are now leaving Skye. Thanks for visiting!" She glanced at it quickly, smiling warmly as it rolled by, then faced forward again, gripping the steering wheel and settling back into her seat.

"Goodbye, Jennifer. Goodbye, Dr. Beecher. You can rest now," she whispered beneath her breath, peace settling over her like a warm blanket. "We all can."

## TO THE READERS

I hope you enjoyed **SECRETS SHE KNEW**. If you did, please leave a review on Amazon, Goodreads, Bookbub, and whatever other social media platforms you enjoy. You can also like, follow and share my pages on Facebook and Twitter found at @dlwoodonline. Reviews and word of mouth are what keep a novelist's work alive, and I would be extremely grateful for yours.

**Would you like a free, award-winning short story?**

Visit my website at www.dlwoodonline.com to subscribe to my newsletter, which will keep you updated (usually only twice a month) on free goodies, giveaways for you, new releases, discounts, advance review team opportunities and more. The short story is my free gift to you for subscribing. While you're there check out my other CleanCaptivingFiction™, including *The Unintended Series* and *The Criminal Collection*.

# WANT MORE SECRETS AND LIES NOVELS?

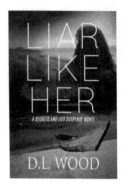

Quinn Bello isn't lying or losing her mind. But when the disbarred attorney discovers a dead body that inexplicably vanishes, no one in her seaside town believes her—no one, that is, except newcomer Ian Wolfe, who for his own mysterious reasons, refuses to hold Quinn's past against her. As they work together to uncover the truth and redeem Quinn's reputation, the danger escalates, along with doubts about Quinn's story, sanity, and ultimately, her innocence. Will Ian and Quinn expose the lies at the heart of the deception before Quinn becomes the next victim? ✱

Get the ebook of *LIAR LIKE HER: A Secrets and Lies Suspense Novel*, available as part of the Dangerous Deceptions Christian Romantic Suspense Boxed Set of 8 novels FOR ONLY 99c.

Preorder now, releases October 2020. (Print version coming November 2020).

# OWN THIS SET OF 8 CHRISTIAN ROMANTIC SUSPENSE NOVELS FOR ONLY 99 CENTS!

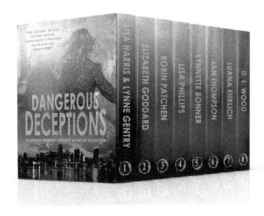

Lives...and hearts...are on the line in eight **brand-new** Christian Romantic Suspense novels from the genre's most explosive authors, including *my* next release...**Liar Like Her: A Secrets and Lies Suspense Novel.** PREORDER NOW FOR ONLY 99c - available for a limited time at all your favorite retailers.

To learn more about all the books and authors included in the set, visit: www.dangerousdeceptions.com

## BONUS EXCERPT FROM
## UNINTENDED TARGET

You don't have to wait until October 2020 to read another D.L. Wood novel. On the following pages is an excerpt from UNINTENDED TARGET, the first novel in *The Unintended Series*, a series with over 2 million pages read on Kindle Unlimited.

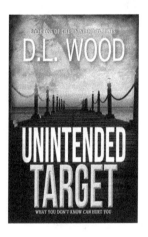

These stories follow Chloe McConnaughey, an unsuspecting travel photojournalist, thrust into harrowing and mysterious circumstances ripe with murder, mayhem, and more. And by more, I mean a handsome man or two that seem too good to be true—and just might be. Turn the page to get started.

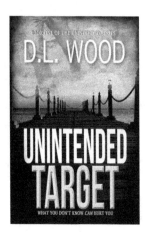

# CHAPTER ONE

"He's done it again," groaned Chloe McConnaughey, her cell
held to her ear by her shoulder as she pulled one final pair of
shorts out of her dresser. "Tate knew that I had to leave by 3:30
at the latest. I sent him a text. I know he got it," she said,
crossing her bedroom to the duffel bag sitting on her four-
poster bed and tossing in the shorts.

Her best friend's voice rang sympathetically out of the
phone. "There's another flight out tomorrow," offered Izzie
Morales hesitantly.

Chloe zipped up the bag. "I know," she said sadly. "But, that
isn't the point. As usual, it's all about Tate. It doesn't matter to
him that I'm supposed to be landing on St. Gideon in six hours.
What does an assignment in the Caribbean matter when your
estranged brother decides it's time to finally get together?"

"Estranged is a bit of a stretch, don't you think?" Izzie asked.

"It's been three months. No texts. No calls. Nothing," Chloe
replied, turning to sit on the bed.

"You know Tate. He gets like this. He doesn't mean anything
by it. He just got . . . distracted," Izzie offered.

"For three months?"

Izzie changed gears. "Well, it's only 3:00—maybe he'll show."

"And we'll have, what, like thirty minutes before I have to go?" Chloe grunted in frustration. "What's the point?"

"Come on," Izzie said, "The point is, maybe this gets repaired."

Chloe sighed. "I know. I know," she said resignedly. "That's why I'm waiting it out." She paused. "He said he had news he didn't want to share over the phone. Seriously, what kind of news can't you share over the phone?"

"Maybe it's so good that he just has to tell you in person," Izzie suggested hopefully.

"Or maybe it's—'I've been fired again, and I need a place to crash.'"

"Think positively," Izzie encouraged, and Chloe heard a faint tap-tapping in the receiver. She pictured her friend on the other side of Atlanta, drumming a perfectly manicured, red-tipped finger on a nearby surface, her long, pitch-colored hair hanging in straight, silky swaths on either side of her face.

"He'll probably pull up any minute, dying to see you," Izzie urged. "And if he's late, you can reschedule your flight for tomorrow. Perk of having your boss as your best friend. I'll authorize the magazine to pay for the ticket change. Unavoidable family emergency, right?"

Chloe sighed again, picked up the duffel bag and started down the hall of her two-bedroom rental. "I just wish it wasn't this hard." The distance between them hadn't been her choice and she hated it. "Ten to one he calls to say he's had a change of plans, too busy with work, can't make it."

"He won't," replied Izzie.

With a thud, Chloe dropped the bag onto the kitchen floor by the door to the garage, trading it for half a glass of merlot perched on the counter. She took a small sip. "Don't underestimate him. His over-achievement extends to every part of his life, including his ability to disappoint."

"Ouch." Izzie paused. "You know, Chlo, it's just the job."

"I have a job. And somehow I manage to answer my calls."

"But your schedule's a little more your own, right? Pressure-wise I think he's got a little bit more to worry about."

Chloe rolled her eyes. "Nice try. But he manages tech security at an investment firm, not the White House. It's the same thing every time. He's totally consumed."

"Well, speaking as your editor, being a *little* consumed by your job is not always a bad thing."

"Ha-ha."

"What's important is that he's trying to reconnect now."

Chloe brushed at a dust bunny clinging to her white tee shirt, flicking it to the floor. "What if he really has lost this job? It took him two years after the lawsuit to find this one."

"Look, maybe it's a promotion. Maybe he got a bonus, and he's finally setting you up. Hey, maybe he's already bought you that mansion in Ansley Park . . ."

"I don't *need* him to set me up—I'm not eight years old anymore. I'm fine now. I wish he'd just drop the 'big-brother-takes-care-of-wounded-little-sister' thing. He's the wounded one."

"You know, if you don't lighten up a bit, it may be another three months before he comes back to see you."

"One more day and he wouldn't have caught me at all."

Izzie groaned jealously. "It's not fair that you get to go and I have to stay. It's supposed to be thirty-nine and rainy in Atlanta for, like, the next month."

"So come along."

"If only. You know I can't. Zach's got his school play next weekend. And Dan would kill me if I left him with Anna for more than a couple days right now." A squeal sounded on Izzie's end. "Uggggh. I think Anna just bit Zach again. I've gotta go. Don't forget to call me tomorrow and let me know how it went with big brother."

"Bigger by just three minutes," she quickly pointed out. "And I'll try to text you between massages in the beach-side cabana."

Izzie groaned again, drowning out another squeal in the background. "You're sick."

"It's a gift," Chloe retorted impishly before hanging up.

Chloe stared down at the duffel and, next to it, the special backpack holding her photography equipment. She double-checked the *Terra Traveler* I.D. tags on both and found all her information still legible and secure. "Now what?" she muttered.

Her stomach rumbled, reminding her that, with all the packing and preparation for leaving the house for two weeks, she had forgotten to eat. Rummaging through the fridge, she found a two-day old container of Chinese take-out. Tate absolutely hated Chinese food. She loved it. Her mouth curved at the edges as she shut the refrigerator door. *And that's the least of our differences.*

Leaning against the counter, she cracked open the container and used her chopsticks to pluck julienne carrots out of her sweet and sour chicken. *Too bad Jonah's not here,* she thought, dropping the orange slivers distastefully into the sink. *Crazy dog eats anything. Would've scarfed them down in half a second.* But the golden retriever that was her only roommate was bunking at the kennel now. She missed him already. She felt bad about leaving him for two whole weeks. Usually her trips as a travel journalist for *Terra Traveler* were much shorter, but she'd tacked on some vacation time to this one in order to do some work on her personal book project. She wished she had someone she could leave him with, but Izzie was her only close friend, and she had her hands full with her kids.

*Jonah would definitely be easier than those two,* she thought with a smile. He definitely had been the easiest and most dependable roommate she'd ever had—and the only male that had never let her down. A loyal friend through a bad patch of three lousy boyfriends. The last of them consumed twelve months of her life before taking her "ring-shopping," only to announce the next day that he was leaving her for his ex. It had taken six months, dozens of amateur therapy sessions with Izzie and exceeding the limit on her VISA more than once to get over that one. After that she'd sworn off men for the fore-seeable future, except for Jonah of course, which, actually, he seemed quite pleased about.

She shoveled in the last few bites of fried rice, then tossed the box into the trash. *Come to think of it,* she considered as she headed for the living room, *Tate'll be the first man to step inside this house in almost a year.* She wasn't sure whether that was empowering or pathetic.

"Not going there," she told herself, forcing her train of thought instead to the sunny beaches of St. Gideon. The all-expenses paid jaunts were the only real perks of her job as a staff journalist with *Terra Traveler,* an online travel magazine based out of Atlanta. They were also the only reason she'd stayed on for the last four years despite her abysmal pay. Photography, her real passion, had never even paid the grocery bill, much less the rent. Often times the trips offered some truly unique spots to shoot in. Odd little places like the "World's Largest Tree House," tucked away in the Smoky Mountains, or the home of the largest outdoor collection of ice sculptures in a tiny town in Iceland. And sometimes she caught a real gem, like this trip to the Caribbean. Sun, sand, and separation from everything stressful. For two whole weeks.

The thought of being stress-free reminded her that at this particular moment, she wasn't. Frustration flared as she thought of Tate's text just an hour before:

*Flying in tonite. Ur place @ 2. Big news. See u then.*

Typical Tate. No advance warning. No, *"I'm sorry I haven't returned a single call in three months"* or *"Surprise, I haven't fallen off the face of the earth. Wanna get together?"* Just a demand.

A familiar knot of resentment tightened in her chest as she took her wine into the living room, turned up Adele on the stereo and plopped onto a slipcovered couch facing the fire. Several dog-eared books were stacked near the armrest, and she pushed them aside to make room as she sank into the loosely stuffed cushions. She drew her favorite quilt around her, a mismatched pink and beige patchwork that melded perfectly with the hodgepodge of antique and shabby chic furnishings that filled the room.

What do you say to a brother who by all appearances has intentionally ignored you for months? It's one thing for two friends to become engrossed in their own lives and lose track of each other for a while. It's something else altogether when your twin brother doesn't return your calls. He hadn't been ill, although that had been her first thought. After the first few weeks she got a text from him saying, *sorry, so busy, talk to u ltr.* So she had called his office just to make sure he was still going in. He was. He didn't take her call that day either.

She tried to remember how many times she'd heard "big news" from Tate before, but quickly realized she'd lost count years ago. A pang of pity slipped in beside the frustration, wearing away at its edges.

She set her goblet down on the end table beside a framed picture of Tate. In many respects it might as well have been a mirror. They shared the same large amber eyes and tawny hair, though she let her loose curls grow to just below her narrow shoulders. Their oval faces and fair skin could've been photo-copied they were so similar. But he was taller and stockier, significantly out-sizing her petite, five foot four frame. She ran a finger along the faint, half-inch scar just below her chin that also differentiated them. He'd given her that in a particularly fierce game of keep-away when they were six. Later, disappointed that she had an identifying mark he didn't, he had unsuccessfully tried duplicating the scar by giving himself a nasty paper cut. In her teenage years she'd detested the thin, raised line, but now she rubbed it fondly, feeling that in some small, strange way it linked her to him.

He had broken her heart more than a little, the way he'd shut her out since taking the position at Inverse Financial nearly a year ago. He'd always been the type to throw himself completely into what he was doing, but this time he'd taken his devotion to a new high, allowing it to alienate everyone and everything in his life.

It hadn't always been that way. At least not with her. They'd grown up close, always each other's best friend and champion. Each other's only champion, really. It was how they survived the day after their eighth birthday when their father, a small-time attorney, ran off to North Carolina with the office copy lady. That was when Tate had snuck into their mother's bedroom, found a half-used box of Kleenex and brought it to Chloe as she hid behind the winter clothes in her closet. *I'll always take care of you, Chlo. Don't cry. I'm big enough to take care of both of us.* He'd said it with so much conviction that she'd believed him.

Together they'd gotten through the day nine months after that when the divorce settlement forced them out of their two-story Colonial into an orange rancher in the projects. Together they weathered their mother's alcoholism that didn't make her mean, just tragic, and finally, just dead, forcing them into foster homes. And though they didn't find any love there, they did manage to stay together for the year and a half till they turned eighteen.

Then he went to Georgia Tech on a scholarship and she, still at a loss for what she wanted to do in life, took odd jobs in the city. The teeny one bedroom apartment they shared seemed like their very own castle. After a couple of years, he convinced her she was going nowhere without a degree, so she started at the University of Georgia. For the first time they were separated. But Athens was only a couple hours away and he visited when he could and still paid for everything financial aid didn't. She'd tried to convince him she could make it on her own, but he never listened, still determined to be the provider their father had never been.

When she graduated, she moved back to Atlanta with her journalism degree under her belt and started out as a copy editor for a local events magazine. Tate got his masters in computer engineering at the same time and snagged a highly competitive job as a software designer for an up-and-coming software development company. It didn't take long for them to recognize Tate's brilliance at anything with code, and the promotions seemed to come one after the other.

Things had been so good then. They were both happy, both making money, though she was only making a little and he, more and more as time went by. The photo in her hands had been taken back then, when the world was his for the taking. Before it all fell apart for him with that one twist of fate that had ruined everything—

*Stop,* she told herself, shaking off the unpleasant memory. The whole episode had nearly killed Tate, and she didn't like to dwell on it. It had left him practically suicidal until, finally, this Inverse job came along. When it did, she thought that everything would get better, that things would just go back to normal. But they didn't. Instead Tate had just slowly disappeared from her life, consumed by making his career work . . .

She brushed his frozen smile with her fingers. Affection and pity and a need for the only person who had ever made her feel like she was a part of something special swelled, finally beating out the aggravation she had been indulging. As she set the frame back on the table, her phone rang.

*Speak of the devil*, she thought, smiling as she reached for her cell.

"Hello?"

A deep, tentative voice that did not belong to her brother answered.

\* \* \* \*

It never ceased to amaze him how death could be so close to a person without them sensing it at all. Four hours had passed and she hadn't noticed a thing. It was dark now, and rain that was turning to sleet ticked steadily on the car, draping him in a curtain of sound as he watched her vague grey shadow float back and forth against the glow of her drawn Roman blinds. He was invisible here, hunkered down across the street behind the tinted windows of his dark Chevy Impala, swathed in the added darkness of the thick oaks lining the neighbor's yard.

Invisible eyes watching. Waiting.

*Watch. Wait.* Simple enough instructions. But more were coming. Out of habit he felt the Glock cradled in his jacket and fleetingly wondered *why* he was watching her, before quickly realizing he didn't care. He wasn't paid to wonder.

He was just a hired gun. A temporary fix until the big guns arrived. But, even so . . .

He scanned the yard. The dog was gone. She was completely alone. *It would be, oh, so easy.*

But he was being paid to watch. Nothing more.

Her shadow danced incessantly from one end of the room to the other. Apparently the news had her pacing.

*What would she do if she knew she was one phone call away from never making a shadow dance again?*

THE STORY CONTINUES IN *UNINTENDED TARGET*
*GET YOUR COPY ON AMAZON NOW*

# ABOUT THE AUTHOR

D.L. Wood is an attorney and best-selling Christian Mystery & Suspense author on Amazon with over three million pages read on Kindle Unlimited. Her books have won multiple awards and offer CleanCaptivatingFiction™ that entertains and uplifts. She loves the art of storytelling, particularly any story involving suspense or the epic struggle of good versus evil. In her novels, Wood tries to give readers the same thing she wants: a "can't-put-it-down-stay-up-till-3am-story" that stays clean without sacrificing an iota of quality, believability or adrenaline.

If she isn't writing, you'll probably catch her curled up with a cup of Earl Grey and her Westies—Frodo and Dobby— bingeing on the latest BBC detective series to show up on Netflix. Speaking of which, if you have one to recommend, please email her immediately, because she's nearly exhausted the ones she knows about. She loves to hear from readers, and you can reach her at dlwood@dlwoodonline.com. D.L. lives in North Alabama with her husband and twin daughters.

Author D.L. Wood's website: www.dlwoodonline.com

facebook.com/dlwoodonline

twitter.com/dlwoodonline

goodreads.com/dlwood

bookbub.com/authors/d-l-wood

amazon.com/D.L.-Wood

# BOOKS BY D.L. WOOD

## The Unintended Series

*Unintended Target*

*Unintended Witness*

*BOOK THREE: COMING 2021*

## The Criminal Collection

*A Criminal Game*

*BOOK TWO: COMING SOON*

## The Secrets and Lies Suspense Novels

*Secrets She Knew*

*Liar Like Her: PRE-ORDER NOW*

as part of the Dangerous Deceptions ebook Boxed Set

of 8 Novels for only 99 cents! *Release Oct 2020.*

*Paperback version coming Nov 2020.*

CPSIA information can be obtained
at www.ICGtesting.com
Printed in the USA
LVHW041510051120
670844LV00002B/340